"And how do I differ from Italian men?"

He seemed genuinely interested in her amateur analysis, and just a little amused.

"You're quieter. You don't wear your emotions on your sleeve. It's very difficult to tell what you're thinking or what your reactions are."

He took another sip of coffee and leaned back in his chair, his eyes on her. "So I'm not like ordinary American men and I'm not like ordinary Italian men. What does that make me?"

Cassie thought about it for a minute. "No ordinary man," she finally said. "You're not like anyone else."

His eyes met hers for a long moment. "Nor are you, Cassandra. Nor are you."

Dear Reader,

Although our culture is always changing, the desire to love and be loved is a constant in every woman's heart. Silhouette Romances reflect that desire, sweeping you away with books that will make you laugh and cry, poignant stories that will move you time and time again.

This summer we're featuring Romances with a playful twist. Remember those fun-loving heroines who always manage to get themselves into tricky predicaments? You'll enjoy reading about their escapades in Silhouette Romances by Brittany Young, Debbie Macomber, Annette Broadrick and Rita Rainville.

We're also publishing Romances by many of your all-time favorites such as Ginna Gray, Dixie Browning, Laurie Paige and Joan Hohl. Your overwhelming reaction to these authors has served as a touchstone for us, and we're pleased to bring you more books with Silhouette's distinctive medley of charm, wit and—above all—*romance*. I hope you enjoy this book, and the many stories to come.

Sincerely,

Rosalind Noonan
Senior Editor
SILHOUETTE BOOKS

SRRL-7/85

BRITTANY YOUNG
No Ordinary Man

Silhouette Romance

Published by Silhouette Books New York

America's Publisher of Contemporary Romance

SILHOUETTE BOOKS
300 E. 42nd St., New York, N.Y. 10017

Copyright © 1985 by Brittany Young

Distributed by Pocket Books

ISBN: 0-373-08388-2

First Silhouette Books printing October 1985

10 9 8 7 6 5 4 3 2 1

America's Publisher of Contemporary Romance

Printed in the U.S.A.

Books by Brittany Young

Silhouette Romance

Arranged Marriage #165
A Separate Happiness #297
No Special Consideration #308
The Karas Cup #336
An Honorable Man #357
A Deeper Meaning #375
No Ordinary Man #388

BRITTANY YOUNG

lives and writes in Racine, Wisconsin. She has traveled to most of the countries that serve as the settings for her Romances and finds the research into the language, customs, history and literature of these countries among the most demanding and rewarding aspects of her writing.

Chapter One

Cassandra Wilde sat behind her father's desk in the comfortable library and studied the young attorney seated across from her with solemn dark blue eyes. "What exactly are you saying, Bill? You seem to be talking all around the problem."

Bill Jordan dropped his professional manner and ran a hand through his thinning hair. His distress was obvious. Cassie had been a friend of his for a long time and he hated having to drop yet another bombshell on her so soon after her father's death.

She leaned forward and touched his hand. "Just say it and get it over with, Bill. Whatever it is, I can take it, believe me."

He shook his head. "It's not good, Cassie. Your father died owing a lot of money."

"My father always owed money."

"But this is different. This is serious. Do you remember four years ago when he started his business as an industrial representative?"

"Of course."

"Well, you had saved up a little money, enough to back your father if he got into trouble, and he talked you into signing some papers to that effect."

"I remember."

Bill got out of his chair and agitatedly paced the room until, as though he couldn't hold back any longer, he stopped in front of the desk and brought his fist down on it. Cassie jumped. "I *told* you not to sign those papers. I warned you that something like this could happen."

Her gaze was steady, but deep inside a feeling of dread was beginning to build. "Something like what?" she asked quietly.

There was a pregnant pause. Then, "You are being held legally responsible for every cent your father owes. He had several silent partners in different parts of the world."

"I know that."

"And another man, an Italian, who as far as I know had no business dealings with your father, has been contacting these men in an attempt to buy up the debts."

That didn't make any sense to Cassie. "Why would anyone do that?"

"I was hoping you could tell me. His name is Franco Luciano. Does that mean anything to you?"

"Franco Luciano," she said thoughtfully. "My godmother's name is Katrina Luciano. He must be a relative of hers. But why would he be asking about my father's debts?''

"*Your* debts, Cassie. Your debts. And I haven't any idea. I have a call in to his office, but so far I haven't heard from him.''

She took a deep breath, dreading the next question, but knowing it had to be asked. "How much do I owe altogether?''

Bill had a page covered with columns of numbers in front of him, and he circled the total and turned the paper toward Cassie. She inhaled sharply and then just stared at it, suddenly feeling ill. "How did my father run up that big a debt? It's impossible.''

"No, it isn't, Cassie,'' he said quietly. "Think about your father's life-style. He diverted funds for his personal use. There's no way around it. My guess is that he gambled most of the money away and spent the rest on women.''

Cassie rubbed her forehead tiredly. "What am I going to do, Bill? Where am I going to get that kind of money?''

"The house and all the land will have to go,'' he told her.

Cassie was heartsick. "But this place has been in our family for three generations!''

"I'm sorry to say it isn't going to see a fourth. And frankly, even if you sell every stick of furniture, every horse, every blade of grass, the money you get will be a fortune by many standards, but it won't cover the whole debt.'' And now he handed her the coup de grace. "There's one more problem, Cassie.''

She looked up in disbelief. What else could there possibly be?

"Your little brother."

"Sam?" she asked, obviously surprised. "What about him?"

The lawyer took some more papers from his brief-case and placed them on the desk before her. "Your father's sister is suing for custody, and, frankly, I think she has a good chance of winning. You're un-married, and even though you're twenty-five and ob-viously responsible enough to raise a seven-year-old boy, I think the courts might be inclined to favor your aunt because of her more stable homelife. And to put it bluntly, you aren't going to have any kind of home at all shortly."

"But I've raised Sam since he was a baby," she protested. "I'm the only mother he's ever had. Aunt Emily has never paid the least attention to him. Why the sudden interest?"

"Because she knows she has an excellent chance at gaining custody if you're her only competition. As I said, you're unmarried, and the courts will look at that very closely. And as for her reason," he shrugged. "In my opinion, she wants control of his trust fund."

"But that's absurd. Even Sam himself can't touch the money in it until he turns twenty-five."

"Ah," he said, leaning forward, "but someone has to manage the trust, and your Aunt Emily wants to be that someone."

Now Cassie understood. "And as Sam's guardian she could, of course, take from the interest on the trust principal whatever she thinks is fair for his expenses."

"Exactly."

With a sigh that started at her toes, Cassie rose from behind the desk and walked over to the big bay window that looked out over the rolling hills of the Illinois estate. She had managed, in one way or another, to handle the problems her father had created in the past. It hadn't always been easy, but her artwork had paid the household bills for years. This was different, though. This time there was no way out.

Bill came up behind her and put his hands on her shoulders. "I wish Kate and I could help you with the money, but we don't have it, and I haven't any idea where we might be able to get it for you. As far as the banks are concerned, you're poison right now."

"As far as the banks are concerned," she said dryly, "anyone who really needs a loan is poison. They only like to hand out their money to people who don't really need it, so they can be sure they'll be paid back."

He gave her shoulders an affectionate squeeze. "I have to get back to the office. If you need me for anything, I'm just a phone call away. Remember that."

She rested her cheek against his hand. "I will."

"And also remember that as long as Kate and I have a home, you have a home. We both love you and Sam."

"I know. Thank you. And give my love to Kate. I haven't talked to her since Father's funeral."

Arm in arm, with the intimacy that comes from knowing someone nearly all your life, they walked to the front door, and then she watched as he drove away, feeling numb. It was impossible to comprehend the magnitude of what was happening to her.

"Hi, Sis," Sam greeted her as he walked out of the kitchen, a sandwich in his hand. "Is Uncle Bill still here?"

"He just left."

The little boy studied his sister with eyes older than his years. "What's wrong?" he finally asked.

Cassie glanced at him in surprise, then put a smile on her face and hunkered down in front of him. Losing both your parents before your eighth birthday was tough enough to handle; she didn't want him to worry about anything else. "Nothing. Why?"

"You're unhappy about something."

She kissed his forehead. "I'm not unhappy. I was just thinking."

"About what?"

"About taking my horse out for a ride," she lied without hesitation. "Want to come with me?"

He studied her for a moment longer, but her smile must have convinced him. "Nope. Can I have some cookies after I finish my sandwich?"

"Two."

"Three?" he asked, hopeful.

"One."

He wrinkled his nose. "All right. Two."

"Good choice." She stood up, but her eyes still rested warmly on him. "I love you, Sam."

He was the picture of seven-year-old embarrassment. "I love you, too."

"Will you be all right here alone for an hour or so?"

"Uh-huh."

"Are you sure?" she asked worriedly.

"I'm *almost* eight," he informed her with pride.

This time her smile was all on the inside. She wouldn't offend his dignity for the world. "A great age, to be sure. I'll be back shortly," she called over her shoulder as she stepped out of the charming old stone house to walk across the well-tended lawn to the stables, some fifty yards away. Her favorite horse, a black stallion named Pharaoh, was in his stall, waiting. She led him out and threw a blanket over his back before hiking up the very feminine white gathered skirt she wore and swinging herself onto his back. He was a tall horse, over seventeen hands. Once astride, she kicked off her shoes, patted the horse's neck and gently pressed against him with her knees. The responsive stallion took off as though he'd been shot from a cannon, knowing the route well. He flew through the open stable doors and over a five-foot white fence in his quest for open pasture. Cassie had been riding since she was four years old, so it was with effortless grace that her body moved with the horse's. Her long, dark hair flew out behind her, and for a while—for just a little while—she left her problems behind.

Franco Luciano turned his rental car into the long drive leading to the Wilde house. It was a beautiful place, but there was more to it than that. It was...comfortable. It looked lived in.

As he parked in front of the house, a boy with a prominent milk mustache and a cookie in his hand walked onto the porch and looked down at him. Franco got out of the car and closed the door. "Hello."

Sam flashed him a friendly smile. "Hi. Who are you?"

Franco returned the smile. "Franco Luciano. And who are you?"

"Sam Wilde." Sam tilted his head to one side and studied the newcomer. "You here to see my sister?"

"I am if her name is Cassandra."

"It is, but she's not here right now." He pointed the cookie in the direction in which she had ridden nearly an hour earlier. "She's out riding. Should be back soon. Wanna wait?"

"Yes, thank you."

The telephone rang and Sam politely excused himself to answer it. Franco started off in the direction in which Sam had pointed. When he got to the fence he put one foot on the bottom rung and waited, his dark-lashed hazel eyes searching the distance. He saw something, but it was just a speck. As he watched, the speck came nearer and began to take on definition, and suddenly Franco found himself mesmerized by the beauty of what he saw: a black stallion, full of unbounded energy, his muscles rippling beneath his coat as he flew across the field, and the woman riding him, her hair, as dark as the stallion, whipping behind her. Her full, white skirt was hiked above her shapely knees and fanned out over the rear of the horse.

Cassie saw him and stopped about twenty yards away. Some instinct told her that this was Franco Luciano, and her heart began a steady beating that she could actually feel beneath the thin material of her blouse. The mystery man had arrived, but what was he here for? Cassie kneed her horse gently and he trotted forward until they reached the fence. Her blue eyes looked directly into the man's hazel ones, but she said nothing.

Franco's eyes traveled over every feature of her face, looking for a flaw and finding none. She was one of the most beautiful women he'd ever seen—all the more so because she seemed so unaware of it. She wore it well, without fuss. "I am Franco Luciano," he said, finally introducing himself.

There was no change in her expression as she leaned forward over the horse's neck and extended her hand. Her shake was firm. "I know," she said in perfectly accented Italian. "I'm Cassie Wilde."

"Your Italian is very good."

"My accent is good. My language skills are adequate."

"Where did you learn it?"

"My mother was Italian—but then, you already knew that." She looked at him curiously. "Who exactly are you in relation to Katrina Luciano?"

"Her grandson."

The stallion moved restlessly. "My attorney tells me that you've been inquiring about the money my father owes."

"Your attorney is well informed."

Cassie waited for him to elaborate, but he didn't seem at all inclined to do so. The stallion stamped his hooves. "I have to get Pharaoh back to the stable. You're welcome to walk along with me."

Franco fell into step beside the woman and the horse.

"I'd join you on the ground," she told him, "but this terrain is kind of unpredictable for bare feet."

His eyes traveled over her shapely, exposed leg to her pretty foot. "Do you always ride in skirts and no shoes?"

She smiled at the question and Franco found himself fascinated by the dimple that played at the corner of her mouth. "I'm unpredictable in that regard. My mother used to tell me I was part gypsy."

When they got to the stables the Italian man caught Cassie off guard by reaching up to place his hands at her waist and lifting her from the saddle. A jolt went through her at his touch, and the surprise she felt at her reaction showed in her eyes. She abruptly stepped away from him.

Sam came running to join them, breathless. "Cassie, my friend Jason just called and asked if I could go to a baseball game with him and his dad tonight and then sleep over. Can I?"

"I don't see why not. What time?"

"He said they'd pick me up in an hour."

"Okay. Would you mind rubbing down Pharaoh for me?"

Sam picked up the horse brush and patted the stallion's silky nose. Suddenly Cassie remembered that Franco was standing there. "I'm sorry," she apologized. "Have you met my brother?"

He winked at Sam. "On the porch, before you returned."

The little boy smiled at him and began to brush the horse. Cassie took Franco's arm and walked out of the cool darkness of the stable into the warm summer day, headed for the house. He was a strong man. She could feel his power through the fingertips she rested gently on his blue-suited arm. "How long have you been in the States?" she asked politely.

"A week."

"Will you be staying awhile longer?"

"I leave for Rome tomorrow evening."

They climbed the porch steps. Cassie glanced at his profile, really looking at him for the first time. He was very attractive, his face a mature one, carved, with a straight Roman nose and well-defined mouth. His hair was dark and straight, parted on one side and combed smoothly away from his face in a very businesslike fashion. And there was a hard edge to him, as though not everything in life had come easily. "Can you stay for dinner?" she found herself asking. There was something about Franco Luciano that piqued her curiosity.

He gazed down at her thoughtfully. In truth, he had other plans, but something drove him to say, "I'd like that, thank you."

As they walked into the house, he looked around the large living room with appreciative eyes. It was as warm and inviting as he had expected. "How long have you lived here?" he asked as he sat on the short couch.

Cassie took the overstuffed chair across from him. "Always. My father inherited it from his parents, and his mother from hers." She gazed around the room and a huge sigh escaped her. It was hard to imagine that someone else would be living here soon. But that was her problem, not his. "I'm going to go upstairs and shower," she said suddenly. "Can I get you something cold to drink first?"

"No, thank you, but I would like to use your telephone."

"Of course. It's in the study, third door down the hall on the right."

He inclined his head and rose when Cassie did. "I won't be long," she told him. His eyes followed her up the stairs until she was out of sight, and then, with his hands in the pockets of his trousers, he walked down the hall and through the open door of the study. He sat behind the desk while he made the call canceling his dinner date and, as he started to rise, his eye was caught by some papers that lay there. He read the first sentence of the petition for custody, then sat down again, picked it up and read it through. When he was finished he read the others, and discovered that even though he had purchased Wilde's debts to his silent partners, there were at least another dozen creditors.

If Jeff Wilde had walked into the room at that moment, Franco would have punched him happily. How could a man with any sense of family responsibility put his children in the position in which he had placed his? It was unconscionable.

Cassie's attractive voice cut through his thoughts. "Hi. Did you make your call?"

He swiveled around in the chair, his dark gaze meeting hers. "I made my call. And then I did a little reading." He inclined his head toward the papers on the desk.

Her smile faded abruptly as she strode across the room and gathered them into a neat pile that she set face down on a corner of the desk. "I thought you were in here to make a phone call, not to go through my personal papers."

"I admit I had no business reading them, but I make no apologies. You're obviously in trouble."

"How astute of you."

He said nothing, but his eyes locked with hers. Cassie's gaze dropped first. "I'm sorry," she said quietly. "The sarcasm was uncalled for. You're absolutely right, of course. I'm in trouble. But it's my trouble and I don't want to discuss it with you. Please."

He started to say something, but Sam came running in at that moment, a backpack slung carelessly across his shoulders. "They're here, Cassie." He kissed her cheek. "See you tomorrow." Then he walked over to Franco and, in a touchingly adult gesture, held out his hand. "It was nice meeting you, Mr. Luciano."

Franco shook the offered hand. "It was nice meeting you, too, Sam."

Then Sam was all little boy again as he ran off. "'Bye!" he yelled over his shoulder. The front door slammed behind him, and Cassie turned her attention back to Franco with a deliberate change of subject. "I thought we'd have steak and salad for dinner, if that's all right with you."

"That sounds fine, Cassie."

She liked the way her name sounded when he said it. His English was perfect, but very formal, and with just the slightest hint of an Italian accent. "Then follow me to the kitchen. You're in charge of the salad."

A corner of his mouth lifted as he rose from behind the desk. No one had ever put him "in charge" of the salad before.

The kitchen was large and open, very bright and clean. Cassie took a bottle of wine from the refrigerator and looked at him with a question in her eyes. "Yes," he answered. "Thank you."

She poured him a glass, and one for herself, then started taking out the things they needed to fix dinner. Franco leaned one powerful shoulder against the wall and watched her, and Cassie was aware that his eyes were on her. Never in her life had she been so conscious of a man's presence. She put the steaks on a wooden board and glanced over at him. "I'm going to put the steaks on the grill. You can start the salad." She went out the back door, and Franco walked over to the counter and searched through the drawers until he found a large knife. He was holding it poised over the lettuce when Cassie's voice stopped him. "No!"

He looked at her over his shoulder. "No?"

She took the knife from his hand and placed it on the counter. "You should never cut lettuce." And then, with the grace and efficiency of a gifted chef, she turned the head of lettuce until she had it where she wanted it, then brought her fist down on the core. The leaves broke away from the core like magic and she lifted it out and tossed it into the sink for the garbage disposal. "Now you take the leaves," she explained, "and tear them by hand." Then she picked up the knife and begain slicing the tomatoes.

"I can see how lettuce would taste better that way," he said, with appropriate solemnity.

Cassie glanced up and met his smiling eyes. A dimple played at the corner of her mouth as they finished the salad in comfortable silence. When the rest of the meal was ready they sat at a small round table set out on the back lawn. The sun was just beginning to go down and the moon was already clearly visible, the warm night breeze lifting Cassie's hair gently away from her neck. The cozy sound of crickets drifted around them.

Franco lifted his glass to Cassie. "Thank you for the nice dinner."

She raised her glass also, and took a sip, wondering what he was thinking.

"You'll find," he told her, seeming to sense her thoughts perfectly, "that I'm not an easy man to read."

Delicate color touched her cheeks as she suddenly concentrated on her steak. "I wouldn't presume to try."

"Liar," he said softly.

She raised her eyes to his and once again blue eyes locked with hazel. Cassie forced hers away. She had to remember that this wasn't a social visit. Signor Franco Luciano was here for a reason. "There's something that's been bothering me ever since my attorney told me about it," she said with admirable nonchalance. "Why have you been contacting the men to whom I owe money?"

He took a leisurely sip of wine and set the glass on the table. "I've done more than contact them. I've purchased their debts. You no longer owe money to your father's former partners."

Cassie studied him curiously, not sure she'd heard right. "I don't understand. Why would you do something like that?"

"Because, as my grandmother's goddaughter, you are my responsibility. This isn't something we take lightly in Italy."

Now she was beginning to understand, but she still didn't believe it. "I owe an enormous amount of money. You don't even know me. And, to be brutally honest, I'm a terrible financial risk at the moment."

"I'm not risking anything, because I don't expect you to pay me back. Consider it a gift from my family to you and Sam."

Cassie was speechless for the first time in recent memory—for a moment. "But I can't let you do that. It's nice of you to want to help us, but..."

"I'm not a nice man, Cassie," he said, cutting through her protest, "and niceness has nothing to do with this. As I've explained, you are my responsibility."

"And as I was trying to tell you before you interrupted," Cassie told him firmly, "thank you, but I can't accept."

Franco studied the woman sitting across from him. Her reaction surprised him. Instead of being grateful, she seemed angry. "All right, then. I've already purchased the debts. What do you propose I do with them?"

The look she flashed him communicated exactly what she proposed he do with them, and a corner of his mouth twitched in acknowledgment. "Perhaps something a bit more biologically feasible," he said.

Cassie's dimple flashed briefly, but then she grew serious again. "You really should have talked with me first. I could have saved you a lot of trouble. As it is, the only thing I can suggest is that you let me pay you back. We'll set up a schedule of some sort so that I can make monthly payments. I'll be selling the house shortly, so that will take care of a substantial portion of what I owe you."

"And how do you propose to pay off the rest?"

"With the money I make from my artwork. For some reason, it seems to have become the 'in' thing the last few years for people to have their portraits done by C. Wilde. It'll never make me rich, but it's been paying the bills around here for a long time."

"You must be very good."

Cassie considered that for a moment. "I think so. I enjoy what I do, and I work hard at it."

Franco took a sip of his wine and leaned back in his chair, his eyes on Cassie. "All right. That takes care of the money, but you still have one very big problem left—Sam."

Cassie suddenly lost her appetite. She set her fork on her plate and pushed it away. "You read everything, I take it?"

"Everything." He leaned forward and poured himself another glass of wine from the bottle on the table. "Your relationship with Sam is more than a sister to a brother, isn't it?"

"Much more," she agreed softly. "It's almost as though he's my own child. I've raised him since I was seventeen."

"Without any help from your father?"

"Without any help from anyone." There was nothing self-pitying in her voice. She was merely stating a fact. Her eyes smiled challengingly into his. "I suppose you can solve my custody problem, too?"

"I can only offer you the solution; the rest is up to you. From what I read, it seems that your aunt's main argument with you as Sam's guardian is the lack of a two-parent family."

"That's right."

"So what you need is to provide Sam with a 'father.'"

"Yes," Cassie said slowly. She had a feeling that she knew what was coming next, but she was stunned when she heard.

"You will marry me."

Her mouth parted softly as her eyes widened. "That's ridiculous. You can't be serious."

"Oh, but I am. It's the only practical solution, and unless there's someone else in your life, marriage to me is the only way you're going to keep Sam."

"But I'm not in love with you!"

"Love has nothing to do with it. This would be a simple business arrangement. If and when you meet someone else or if you can work out an agreement with your aunt, the marriage can be annulled."

"Just like that."

"Just like that," he agreed.

Cassie sat back in her chair and shook her dark head. "This is extraordinary. I've never even met your grandmother, and here you are, willing to give up your freedom simply because twenty-five years ago my mother asked Katrina Luciano to stand as my godmother."

"Don't misunderstand me, Cassie. I'm involved with another woman, and marriage to you will not alter that. This is strictly a matter of convenience for you, and I see no reason to pretend otherwise, publicly or privately."

"It sounds so cold-blooded," she said softly.

"And so it is. There's nothing wrong with that, as long as it's clearly understood by both of us beforehand." He watched her for a moment. "So what's your answer?"

Cassie lowered her eyes to her lap and watched her hand as it automatically smoothed the linen napkin over and over again. Her heart ached. How could her life have changed so drastically in a matter of weeks? She had always been so independent, but that was a luxury she could no longer afford. At least, not if she wanted to keep Sam. This man—this cool, detached stranger—had offered Cassie a lifeline and she had no choice but to take it and try to make the best of a bad situation. She took a deep breath and slowly exhaled, then raised her eyes to his. "My answer is yes. How long do you think we'll have to stay married?"

"Until the judge in the case signs the documents granting you permanent custody."

"How long do you suppose that will take?"

"Anywhere from three weeks to three months."

"And then what?"

"Then we get the marriage annulled and go our separate ways."

Just like that. And why not? she thought as she picked up her wineglass and tossed back its contents. "I'll make some coffee," she said quietly, as she picked up their dinner plates and carried them into the kitchen. Franco's enigmatic eyes followed her into the house and then watched through the large window as she made the coffee. His wife-to-be had a great deal of innate dignity. He liked that. But behind those eyes rested a mischievous spirit. He liked that, too. He knew how difficult this was for her, but he couldn't help that. It was something she was going to have to deal with.

Suddenly he rose and went into the house. "I've changed my mind about the coffee. I have some things

I need to take care of this evening, and I think you can probably use some sleep. It's been a long day."

Cassie cleared her throat and turned. It was incredibly difficult, but she managed a small smile. "Of course."

His eyes met hers for a long moment. "Good night, Cassie," he finally said as he turned to go.

"Good night."

She stood very still after he had gone and listened as his car drove away. Then she mechanically cleaned up the kitchen and walked around the house, turning out the lights.

She didn't even bother to undress when she finally got to her room, but lay down fully clothed on top of the bedspread, her hands behind her head, staring up at the ceiling. She was physically and emotionally drained. And she was a little ashamed because, mixed in with her hurt pride and frustration at her helplessness, was a certain relief. She didn't have to worry about losing Sam anymore, and she didn't have to worry about the money she owed. She could pay Franco back when she was able to. For the first time in her life, someone else was taking care of things for her.

With a tired sigh, her eyes slowly drifted closed.

Franco pulled his car off to the side of the road and sat there, perfectly still, for a long time. He had actually asked a woman he'd known for only a few hours to marry him. And deep in his soul he knew the reason went deeper than Cassie's relationship to his grandmother. It was Cassie herself. Something about her....

But the timing was all wrong. He was involved in prosecuting a prominent underworld figure in Rome. One of the worst things he could do right now was show up with a wife and child in tow. Franco couldn't guarantee his own safety, much less theirs. About all he could do was hope the estate would take a long time to sell. There might be no need for the two of them to come to Italy at all.

He rubbed his forehead tiredly before putting his car into gear and pulling back onto the highway.

Chapter Two

Cassie woke early the next morning and couldn't get back to sleep. She focused on the ceiling and tried to think through what was happening in her life, but found that she couldn't concentrate. For someone who was used to meeting life's problems head-on, this was a strange experience.

Perhaps the answer was not to think about it at all, and hope for the best. What she needed was something physical to do to use up her nervous energy. Cassie quickly climbed out of bed and donned a pair of jeans and an old shirt. She pulled her dark hair away from her face and caught it in a ponytail, then went downstairs and pulled out the vacuum cleaner and ran it through every room in the house—which was no small feat. When that was done she got out the furniture polish and rubbed until her shoulders ached with the effort.

When the last piece of furniture was sparkling she turned her attention to the kitchen and scrubbed the floor, but still she felt jumpy, so when that was clean she went outside and started digging in the flower beds. It was a very warm day, and the heat was mixed with just enough humidity to make it really uncomfortable. After only a few minutes her shirt was sticking to her back with perspiration. Still holding a trowel, she raised the back of her hand to wipe away the beads of sweat, leaving a streak of dirt behind.

Franco, his steps muffled by the grass, walked up behind her and stood watching her feverish activity. "Good morning," he said.

Cassie gasped and the trowel flew from her hand to land about six feet away.

Franco gazed down at her with eyes tinged with surprisingly gentle amusement. "I'm sorry. I didn't mean to frighten you. Are you all right?"

She took a shaky breath. "That depends. Just how important *is* the heart?"

The grooves in his cheeks deepened as he reached out a hand to help her to her feet. She accepted it only briefly, then bent over to brush the dirt from her knees. When she straightened, Franco took out a handkerchief and wiped the streak from her cheek. "Nice day, don't you think?" she asked self-consciously as she waited for him to finish, once again amazed at her awareness of his slightest touch.

A corner of his mouth lifted. "This is awkward, isn't it?"

She was grateful for his understanding. "Thank you for stopping me before I went into any meteorological detail."

His eyes moved over her lovely, flushed face. "I've arranged for a judge to come here in about an hour to perform the ceremony. There are some papers you need to sign, but that shouldn't take too long."

Cassie's heart lurched, but she managed to maintain an outward calm. "So soon? I haven't had a chance to explain things to Sam...."

"It has to be today, Cassie," he said quietly. "I'm leaving for Rome early this afternoon."

Cassie pulled the band out of her ponytail and ran her fingers through her dark hair. "Am I supposed to leave with you? I have a lot to do here with getting the house ready for sale. Things have to be packed, and furniture auctioned off."

"Take all the time you want. You needn't come until everything here is settled."

A wave of relief washed over her.

At that moment Sam came running around the side of the house. "There you are! I've been looking all over for you."

Franco saw Cassie's face light up as she caught him in her arms. "Did you have a good time?"

"It was great!" He turned to Franco. "Hello, Mr. Luciano," he said politely, then turned back to his sister. "The Cubs won, and then we cooked hot dogs on the grill for dinner and slept in sleeping bags in the backyard. Jason's dad told us ghost stories."

"It sounds like you had fun." Cassie looked up at Franco, as though asking for guidance, and then back at Sam. She took a deep breath. "Sam, you and I need to have a talk."

Franco moved behind Cassie and rested his hands lightly on her shoulders. "The three of us need to have a talk."

Sam's smile faded a little. "What about?"

Cassie turned her head slightly and looked up at Franco, waiting for him to answer.

His hands pressed her shoulders a little harder, silently telling her not to worry. It was a surprisingly comforting gesture, and Cassie suddenly discovered that this stranger who had come so abruptly into her life had a human side. "Your sister and I are going to be married."

Sam blinked. "Married? You mean you're going to be living here?" he asked the man.

"No. I mean you're going to live with me in Italy. Not immediately, but sometime in the next few months."

The boy's eyes grew wide. "Italy! Wow! Do you have a chariot?"

"Sam watches a lot of television," Cassie explained dryly.

The grooves in Franco's cheeks deepened. "Only the kind with an engine."

Sam wrinkled his nose. "Oh, well. I suppose it'll be neat there anyway. Can I have something to eat?" he asked his sister.

Cassie couldn't believe how casually he was taking the most earthshaking news of her life. "Anything but cookies." He ran into the house and she turned to Franco. "He doesn't seem too traumatized by the news."

"Unlike his sister."

Cassie's dark blue eyes searched his carved face. "I'm not traumatized. Just a little scared. I don't know you and you don't know me, and in just about thirty minutes we're going to be married."

Franco said nothing, but his gaze grew in intensity until Cassie had to lower her eyes. "I should get ready." She headed for the back door, but stopped suddenly and turned. "I forgot to say thank you last night. I know I've seemed something less than grateful, but I really do appreciate what you're doing for Sam and me." She felt his eyes follow her the rest of the way.

Twenty minutes later she stood wrapped in a towel in front of her closet, staring at her clothes. It was hard to imagine that she was looking for something to be married in.

Finally she pulled out a white skirt and blouse and held them against her, still on the hangers and critically examined herself in the mirror. Not fancy, but nice, she finally decided. And strangely, sham marriage or not, it was important to her that she wear white.

After she was dressed she put on a little makeup, and then brushed her dark, shoulder-length, blunt-cut hair and left it alone. It was a simple style that suited her.

As she studied her reflection, she heard Franco's voice. She went into the hall and leaned over the railing to look at the man standing below.

"The judge is here."

Her heart stopped, then started beating again. "I'll be right down." She moved away from the railing so that he couldn't see her and took a deep breath. Then she pulled her shoulders back, raised her chin, walked to the top of the staircase and slowly descended. When she reached the bottom Franco held out his arm, and she lightly placed her hand on it. He said nothing, but Cassie sensed that he liked the way she looked.

A tall, thin man stood in the living room, looking appropriately serious. Two women stood behind him—undoubtedly the witnesses. Sam sat quietly on the couch and watched as Cassie and Franco took their places in front of the judge and repeated their vows. Franco placed a narrow gold band on her finger. "You may kiss the bride," the judge intoned.

Franco turned to her. His hazel eyes rested on her pale face for a long moment before he kissed her forehead lightly and impersonally. "It's time to take me to the airport."

A week later Cassie was walking through her house with a real estate broker and a middle-aged couple. She could tell the woman liked it, but she couldn't figure out what the man was thinking until they had finished the tour and were standing in the foyer. "We'll take it."

Both Cassie and the broker were speechless. No one bought a house that quickly.

"I want the furniture, too. It suits the house. Of course I'll add an appropriate amount to the purchase price to cover that."

"But there are papers to be filled out and…" the broker began.

"The only papers I want anything to do with are the final purchase documents. As far as I'm concerned,

I've made a verbal offer and I'll stand by it. How soon can we close?''

The broker looked at Cassie. "What do you think?''

Frankly, she was shocked. The property was an expensive one, and she had expected it to be on the market for months, not days. This was her home—the only one she'd ever known—and once it was sold, that was it.

But it had to be done. Cassie swallowed hard, then forced the words from her lips. "I accept the offer."

The broker nodded. "Then we can have the closing within the week, as long as there are no financing complications.''

"There won't be," the man said confidently.

She believed him. As soon as the couple had gone, the broker hugged her jubilantly. "This is wonderful! They've been looking at houses for over a year, but I had a feeling this was the one they'd buy the minute you called me to put it on the market. I'll get the ball rolling as soon as I get back to the office." And then she left, too.

Cassie went into the living room and sank onto the couch. Her eyes roamed sadly, resting on this piece of furniture and that picture. The deed was done. As soon as everything was legal, she would take the check to Italy and present it to Franco. It wouldn't pay off the debt, but it would certainly help.

The plane Cassie and Sam were on landed at the Rome airport two weeks later. After clearing a very perfunctory customs check, she led a sleepy Sam to a taxi and settled into the backseat while the driver loaded their luggage into the trunk. Then he climbed in and looked at her, a question in his eyes. Cassie took a piece of paper from her purse and read Franco's address to him in Italian. "It's not far," he told her in heavily accented English as he put the car into gear and pulled into traffic. "Twenty-five kilometers."

Cassie glanced at Sam. "How are you doing, sport?"

He yawned and stared out the window. "Okay, but I'm tired."

Cassie smiled softly. Sam never admitted to being tired unless he was ready to drop in his tracks. "We should be at the villa soon. You can go to bed as soon as we get there."

He yawned again. With a smile tugging at her mouth, Cassie relaxed and watched the scenery fly by the window. And it did fly. The driver weaved in and out of the evening traffic, enthusiastically honking his horn and making vigorous hand motions at the other drivers. At one point he had to wait for a woman to cross the street, and he beseeched the gods to tell him why he should be the one chosen to endure these delays. As soon as she was past his car, he slammed into gear, tires squealing on the pavement as he shot forward.

The airport was a considerable distance from the city of Rome itself, and Cassie saw with some disappointment that they wouldn't be going through the center of Rome to get to Franco's home, but around it, and into the countryside.

The beautiful countryside. Cassie was enchanted by the occasional sight of elegant Roman villas silhouetted against the dusky evening sky.

It was some time later that they turned onto a mile-long private drive, stunningly lined with tall, stately cypress trees. Franco's villa loomed at the end of that drive, and Cassie's first sight of it left her speechless. It was large, but not overpoweringly so, and built in a U shape, open in the middle to accommodate a courtyard. Columns with scrolled capitols, spaced at five-foot intervals, extended across the portico. The large windows, particularly on the upper story, were covered by even larger wooden shutters to keep out the intense afternoon sun. More cypress trees lined the outer walls of the villa and stretched above the roof.

Only a few lights shone in the windows. "Do you suppose anyone's home?" she asked her brother.

There was no answer.

"Sam?" Cassie looked over and found him sound asleep. She reached out a gentle hand and pushed the dark hair from his forehead. "Would you mind waiting here for just a moment?" she asked the taxi driver as he stopped in front of the villa. "I won't be long."

Wearily, she climbed out of the taxi and made her way to the large double front doors. She smoothed her travel-weary clothes and took a deep breath before knocking. A man opened the door almost immediately, as though he were on his way out. He pulled up short and looked her over with appreciative eyes. She must have appeared as American as she was, because he spoke to her in English. "Well, hello there. What can I do for you?"

"I'm looking for Franco Luciano."

"I am his brother, Taddeo. Will I do?"

Cassie couldn't help smiling. "Not this time, thank you. Would you please tell him that Cassandra Wilde is here?'' She wasn't even aware that she hadn't used her married name. She didn't feel married.

His eyes widened appreciatively. "So you're Cassandra."

At least he'd heard of her, that was a start. "Is Franco here?"

"No, I'm afraid not. He's having a dinner party at his apartment in Rome tonight. As a matter of fact—" he glanced down at his tuxedo "—that is where I was just about to go."

"I see." Tiredness was evident in her voice. And there was a touch of disappointment, too. She hadn't realized until that moment that she'd actually been looking forward to seeing Franco again. The knowledge made her a little uncomfortable.

Taddeo suddenly remembered his manners and stepped away from the door. "Please, come in."

She glanced back at the waiting taxi. "My little brother is asleep in the taxi. I'd appreciate it if someone could carry him to his room without waking him. He's had a long trip."

Taddeo inclined his head. "I will see to it myself. Wait here, please." He walked to the taxi and spoke briefly to the driver before handing him some money. The driver then got out the luggage, and Taddeo picked up Sam and carried him into the house. Cassie followed him through the wide marble foyer and up a curving staircase while the taxi driver brought up the rear with some of the luggage.

A heavy woman dressed in a maid's crisp uniform, gesturing wildly with her hands and speaking Italian too rapidly for Cassie to follow, came running to meet them and blocked the stairway, standing facing them with her hands on her ample hips. Taddeo looked at Cassie and shook his head. "Maria thinks you're one of my disreputable women."

"Who does she think Sam is?"

"One of my disreputable women's disreputable children." He turned back to the maid and lifted his hand in a quick gesture that silenced her. Then, in much slower Italian so that Cassie could follow, he introduced Cassie to the maid. Maria's eyes widened as she stared at Cassie, and her attitude changed instantly into one of helpfulness. She led the way to a room down the hall that had been prepared for Sam. It was large and airy and seemed to have been occupied by a child in years past. There were even toys. Taddeo laid the child on the bed and Cassie took off his shoes before covering him with a blanket. Sam slept on, oblivious to everything and everyone.

Then they went to Cassie's room. The shutters were open on the floor-to-ceiling windows, allowing a fresh breeze to gently lift the creamy curtains. A large canopied bed, covered in material that was the same color as the curtains, caught Cassie's attention. The room was decorated in a rich shade of cream, kissed with a hint of peach to give it warmth. A couch and chairs were set up in a conversational grouping near the windows. Rather than a closet, there was a large armoire in which to hang her clothes.

Taddeo cleared his throat to get her attention, and Cassie turned with a friendly smile. "Thank you."

"My pleasure, pretty lady."

Maria bustled around the room, telling the taxi driver where to put the luggage and then shooing him out the door. Taddeo still stood there, looking at Cassie. "How long will it take you to get dressed?"

She looked at him in surprise. "Dressed for what?"

"The dinner party."

Cassie shook her head. "No. No, I couldn't." She moved out of the maid's way as Maria, speaking to herself in a nonstop stream of Italian, hoisted one of her suitcases onto the bed and began unpacking. "Franco isn't expecting me and it wouldn't be right to simply show up."

"Don't be ridiculous. You're family."

This was incredibly awkward.

Taddeo seemed to sense it and took her hand in his, raising it briefly to his mouth. "Look, I know the story behind the marriage. And thanks to me, so does everyone else. But the fact remains that technically you're a Luciano right now. Family. If my brother had known you were coming today he would have invited you himself."

Maria pulled out a beautiful, sunshine-yellow satin dress Cassie had packed in her suitcase, and draped it over the end of the bed. Taddeo looked at it and then back at Cassie. "That would be perfect." And before Cassie could say anything, he lifted his hand in a little wave and excused himself. "I'll be back for you in twenty minutes."

Cassie was amused by his persistence, but unfortunately it didn't relieve any of her tiredness. She turned to her suitcase and tried to help Maria with the unpacking, but the maid seemed to take it as a personal affront and waved her away.

A few minutes later Maria closed the now empty suitcase and removed it from the bed. "Can I do any-

thing else for you? Bring you anything?'' she asked
Cassie in Italian.

"No, thank you. But I would appreciate it if you
would look in on Sam while I'm gone this evening."
Cassie, too, spoke in Italian.

Maria bobbed her head and left. Then Cassie, after
one more longing glance at her bed, showered and got
ready for the party. The dress she had packed so carefully in her suitcase was one of her favorites. The pale
yellow color emphasized her dark hair and pale skin,
just as the tight bodice with its dropped waist and skirt
that flared out to just above her knees emphasized
her seductively slender figure. Her heart wasn't in her
preparations, though, and rather than sweeping her
hair up, she let it fall to her shoulders. She finished
with a touch of makeup and simple pearl earrings,
then stood away from the mirror to examine herself.
Even the makeup didn't entirely mask her weariness,
but Franco would have no reason to be embarrassed
by her.

With a last look at her reflection, she took a deep
breath and headed downstairs. Taddeo stood waiting
for her in the foyer. He looked her up and down very
thoroughly, but managed to do it without being of-
fensive. "I wish Franco had called me about your
needing a husband. I would have volunteered
happily."

Cassie's quick smile lit her face. "Thank you."

He held out his arm to her and they went outside to
his waiting car. Darkness had overtaken the dusk. A
few minutes later they were off the private property
and on the highway. Cassie felt Taddeo's eyes on her
every now and then, and she knew he wanted to talk,

but she had too much on her mind. Her stomach was in a knot over seeing Franco again. She willed herself to relax, but it didn't work. She felt like a teenager about to go out on her first date. What should she say? How should she act?

Suddenly Taddeo reached over and rested his hand on her clenched ones. "It's all right, Cassie. Franco won't bite you."

She smiled at his brotherly gesture. "I know. I'll be fine."

The traffic in the city was still heavy. Taddeo explained that Italians kept strange hours. They usually closed their businesses for several hours in the afternoon and then opened them again in the evenings. Dinner was rarely eaten before nine o'clock. And then there was the parking problem. Cars were everywhere. The streets of Rome had not been planned to handle anywhere near the number of automobiles that raced through them every day, and parking places were nearly nonexistent. Taddeo pulled his car onto a wide sidewalk in front of an old building that looked as though it held two large apartments, both with upper-story terraces. Then he helped Cassie out and walked her inside. It was innocuous enough in the hallway and stairwell as they walked up one flight.

Taddeo knocked on the door and a servant answered, then stood aside for them to enter. Cassie's eyes opened wide. The apartment was beautiful. Prohibitively expensive works of art hung casually on the walls. The servant led them through several rooms filled with people until they reached the one where Franco stood talking with a group of men. Cassie's eyes went directly to Franco, as though some sixth sense pointed her gaze. She stared at the back of his head, noticing that his hair was a little long in back and touched the white collar of his shirt.

A dramatic-looking red-haired, dark-eyed woman came to Taddeo and put her hand on his arm, but her eyes were on Cassie. "Taddeo, I'm so glad you could come. Who is this?"

Taddeo suddenly seemed uneasy. "Adriana, what are you doing here? I thought you were in Paris."

"And so I was, until today. And so I will be again after tomorrow, though just for a week." She held her hand out to Cassie in a friendly gesture. "Hello. I'm Adriana Simoni."

Cassie knew without anyone telling her that this was the woman with whom Franco was involved. At this point she had no choice but to brave the situation out. "How do you do? I'm Cassandra Wilde."

The woman's eyes widened in surprise. "You?"

Cassie felt ill. This was very embarrassing. "And I owe you an enormous apology for intruding this evening," she continued with quiet dignity. "Ordinarily, I'd wish for the earth to open up and swallow me whole, but there doesn't seem much chance of that happening, so I'll just ask Taddeo if he'd be kind enough to drive me back to the villa." She turned to leave, but Franco's deep voice cut across the room.

"Cassie."

Her heart stopped at the sound of his voice. She took a deep breath and slowly exhaled before turning back. Dark blue eyes locked with hazel as he moved across the room until he stood in front of her. Despite all the tension, she noticed how well the white jacket fit his broad-shouldered frame. "What are you doing here?"

Cassie glanced dryly at Taddeo. "Strange you should ask."

Taddeo rolled his eyes heavenward and moved to her side. "This is all my fault, Franco. I'll take her home."

"No," he said quietly, his eyes still on Cassie. "You stay here with Adriana and the guests and I'll take her back to the villa."

Without another word to anyone, he put his hand on the small of Cassie's back and led her outside to a black Ferrari, helped her in and climbed behind the wheel. The top was down, and as he put the car in motion, Cassie decided she just wasn't going to be embarrassed anymore. With a sigh, she closed her eyes and rested her head against the seat, letting the cool night air blow against her face.

"When did you arrive in Italy?"

She turned her head and stared at his profile. "This evening. The house and property sold more quickly than I expected, and the people who bought it wanted immediate occupancy. Sam and I had nowhwere to go but here."

"Is Sam at the villa?"

"With Maria. Sound asleep."

She saw a corner of his mouth lift. "I like Sam. He's a nice boy."

"He likes you, too. He was excited about seeing you again."

The city streets gave way to open highway. In Italy there was no such thing as a speed limit, and Franco took full advantage of that fact, but with such skill that Cassie wasn't at all nervous as the night lights of the dark countryside flashed by.

She must have sighed again without realizing it, because Franco said, "You sound tired yourself."

"I am. The past few weeks have seemed longer than the entire twenty-five years of my life." She felt his eyes on her and turned her head to meet his gaze. "I really am sorry about this evening. I should never have let Taddeo talk me into coming."

He looked back at the road. "He didn't know Adriana would be there, and there's no need for you to apologize. It was unfortunate, but Adriana understands the situation."

"Good. I wouldn't want to be the cause of any friction."

"I didn't say there wasn't any friction," he said dryly.

For the first time in days, Cassie actually laughed, and it felt good. They grew silent as they drove down the long road to the villa. Franco pulled up by the front door, walked around the car and held out his hand to help Cassie out. She hesitated—but only for a moment—before putting her hand in his. Any physical contact with him made her feel strangely jumpy.

When they were inside the first thing he did was take off his jacket and toss it over a chair in the foyer. One sharp tug of his bow tie had it hanging in two strips down his chest. "Aren't you going back?" Cassie asked as she watched.

"Yes, but not right now. Have you had dinner?"

"No."

He took her hand and walked her through the villa until they reached the kitchen. It was a modern one, and very large, with a small table set in a nook. With his hands at her waist, Franco hoisted Cassie onto the counter and started pulling out bowls and skillets. "What would you like in your omelet?"

"Cheese, I suppose," she answered, frowning a little. "What about your dinner party?"

"They will have eaten by the time I get back, and I'm too hungry to go without dinner tonight." He cracked some eggs into a bowl and handed it to her, along with a whisk. While she beat the eggs, Franco grated some cheese and heated butter in a skillet.

Cassie followed his movements with surprise. This was a man who obviously knew his way around a kitchen. "Where did you learn to cook?"

"All Italian men know how to cook—even if not how to prepare lettuce." There was a smile in his voice. He took the bowl from her and poured the beaten eggs into the skillet, then came back to Cassie and lifted her off the counter. "The plates are over there," he said, pointing to a cupboard, "the silverware there and glasses and napkins over there."

By the time she'd finished setting the table the omelet was ready. Franco folded it onto a plate, cut it down the middle and slid half of it onto her plate. Then he poured them each a glass of red wine. His eyes met hers in a long look, and he raised his glass to her. "You look beautiful tonight, Cassie. I hope that when this comedy we're playing has ended, you find a man worthy of you." The look in his eyes took her breath away.

"Thank you. Though I'd be glad to settle for some peace of mind. Men don't necessarily give you that."

Franco looked away as he drank.

Cassie watched him curiously. "What is it that you want to say to me, but haven't yet?"

His eyes met hers. "You're very observant."

Cassie waited.

"I'd like you to think about staying somewhere else for a few weeks. This is a bad time for you to be here. I have a friend in Switzerland who would be more than happy to have the two of you as guests...."

Cassie's shoulders straightened automatically, though her heart sank. There were no words to describe the humiliation she felt at being dependent on someone else, particularly when she and Sam were such an obvious burden. "Of course. I understand. We'll go wherever you want."

There was something about the way her voice deepened that caught his attention. Franco reached across the table and raised her eyes to his with a gentle finger beneath her chin. "What's the matter?"

Her lips parted softly to answer, but then she changed her mind, afraid she wouldn't be able to get the words out without tears. She set her fork down and dabbed at her mouth with her napkin. "Nothing," she finally managed as she rose and carried her plate to the counter. "If you don't mind, I'd like to go to my room now."

She felt Franco behind her before he placed his hands on her shoulders and turned her to face him. "I do mind. Talk to me, Cassie."

She drew in a shaky breath, trying hard to stave off the tears that were so near. "I can't." The words were little more than a whisper. "You wouldn't understand." A tear slipped down her cheek and Cassie dashed it away with the back of her hand, annoyed by her show of weakness.

Franco softened visibly. She had been so stoic about everything in Illinois. "I just might, Cassie. Try me."

She took another deep breath and then several more shallow ones. She wanted to lower her eyes, but she forced herself to look directly at Franco. "I," she began, and then stopped, cleared her throat and tried again. "I'm angry," she finally managed. "With my father for dying when he was so deeply in debt; with myself for being trusting enough to sign papers that made me legally responsible for paying back those debts; with the nice couple who bought Sam's and my home, because they can never love it the way we did; with my aunt for trying to take Sam away from me...." She paused. "And with you," she said softly. "I think most of all with you. I'm completely in your debt, and while I'm grateful for the way you rescued Sam and me—" she shook her head "—there's a part of me that hates you for it. How's that for being irrational?"

He wrapped his arms around Cassie and pulled her comfortingly against his powerful body. His chin rested on her silky head, and a small ache grew inside her; it felt so good to be held. "There's nothing wrong with what you're feeling, and there's certainly nothing irrational about it. You resent the loss of the control you've always had over your life. I'd feel the same way." He held her slightly away from himself and gazed curiously into her eyes. "But what was it about my asking you to go to Switzerland that set you off?"

Cassie lifted her shoulders. "I suppose it was because, for the first time, I realized exactly what a burden you'd taken on when you married me."

His eyes crinkled attractively at the corners. "You think I want you out of sight somewhere in Switzerland because you're a burden?"

"Why else?"

"Because your life—yours much more than Sam's—could be in danger in Italy right now."

"That's absurd. Who would want to hurt me?"

"Not you. Me."

Now she was really confused.

"You don't even know what I do for a living, do you?"

It wasn't until he asked the question that Cassie realized how little she knew about him. "We've never talked about it, no."

"I'm an attorney. I have a private practice, but most of my work is as a special prosecutor for the Italian government against certain types of criminals."

"Are you talking about the Mafia?"

"Yes. Them and the terrorists who seem to thrive in Italy."

She leaned against the counter. "I take it that you're prosecuting someone right now?"

"A man named Genco. He's an important mob figure in Rome. The trial starts in a few weeks."

"And you think that this person on trial, this Genco, might try to get to you by harming me."

"It's happened before. Not to me, but to other prosecutors. Even judges. And that's why I'd like you to consider going to Switzerland until either the trial is over or the papers are signed granting you custody of Sam.''

"All right," she agreed. "I'll think about it."

"Good. And now I'll take you to your room. I have to get back to my apartment."

She turned her eyes away from him and looked straight ahead as they walked. "Does Adriana live there?" she asked casually.

A corner of his mouth lifted. "No."

Cassie didn't try to explain to herself the relief she felt.

"Which room did Maria put you in?"

Cassie pointed up the stairs. "Down the hall, second door on the right."

He shook his head. "I explained the situation to her. I don't know why she did that."

"Did what?"

"Put you in a room connected to mine. If you want to change, I'll arrange to have your things moved."

She was feeling much more relaxed with him than she had earlier. "That's not necessary. I mean, if a woman can't trust her husband, who can she trust?" she asked with a quick smile. Then she put her hand on his arm. "You go on back to your party. I can find my way from here."

Franco's thoughtful gaze followed her up the stairs. She was different than he'd expected her to be. He liked her. He liked talking with her.

Still thoughtful, he picked up his jacket and carried it, hooked on a finger, over his shoulder as he left the villa.

When she got to her room Cassie slipped out of her dress and hung it neatly in the armoire. Maria had gotten out her white silk nightgown and had placed it neatly across the turned-down bed. Cassie picked it up and held it against her. It was really beautiful, but completely inappropriate. With a sigh, she put it away and took out a blue football jersey that reached to just above her knees and slipped it over her head.

Then she climbed between the covers of her wonderfully comfortable bed, reached over to turn out the lamp and sank back against the pillows. Heaven.

Several hours later she was awakened by the sound of a door closing and movement in the next room. Cassie raised herself up on an elbow and looked at the crack beneath the door that connected her room to Franco's. There was a dim light. She lay back and stared at the ceiling as she smoothed the sheet over and over with her right hand, wide awake. There wasn't a chance in the world that she was going to fall back asleep. Without really thinking about what she was doing, she padded, barefoot, across her room and knocked on the door.

"Come."

When she opened the door her eyes searched the shadowy room. Franco's tuxedo jacket had been tossed carelessly over the back of a chair. A movement near one of the windows caught her attention. Franco stood there, one shoulder against the frame as he stared outside, a brandy snifter in his hand. Cassie moved farther into the room. "Hi."

He turned his head slightly and looked at her for a long moment. "Hello."

She hesitated. "I woke up and couldn't get back to sleep."

"That's not surprising."

"No, I suppose not. May I sit down?"

He gestured toward a chair near his bed and Cassie curled herself onto it. "I did some thinking about going to Switzerland."

He looked at her and waited.

"I'd rather stay here."

He didn't show any disappointment. "All right."

"And I'd like to try to be of some help to you."

"No free rides?"

Cassie smiled. "Something like that."

Franco set the snifter down and began unfastening the studs in his shirt. "What did you have in mind?"

"I really don't know. I was hoping you'd have some suggestions."

When his shirt was completely unfastened except for the part that was still tucked into his trousers, he retrieved the snifter and stretched out on the bed, one hand behind his head. "I haven't really thought about this arrangement of ours, beyond giving you and Sam a temporary home. What are some of the things you'd be comfortable doing?"

"I'm good at organizing a household."

"I have a housekeeper."

"Oh." She thought some more. "I'm a good cook."

"I have a cook."

"Oh." She studied him even as he looked at her. Franco Luciano was a very attractive man. Even lying there perfectly still, he radiated power. "Then I guess it's time to pull out my big guns."

He lifted a dark brow.

"I play the piano well, mostly classical; I've been told that I'm a good hostess; I mix a mean martini and know what wines go with what foods; I'm a very competitive chess player..."

Franco, his eyes warmed by a smile, lifted his hand to stop her. "I'm sure we can put some of those qualities to good use. It's too bad you can't type, though," he said regretfully.

"And I can type," she finished. "I needed something to fall back on in case my painting didn't work out."

Franco's teeth flashed white in his dark face. "A woman who covers all the bases. I like that."

Cassie inclined her head.

Then he grew more serious. "What I really need you to do if you're to stay here is to be independent and to mind your own business. There are going to be times when things happen that you won't understand, and you're going to have to accept them without asking questions."

"I'll try."

Cassie started to rise, but Franco waved her back in the chair and sat on the edge of the bed, facing her. "I made a decision tonight that I think you should know about."

Cassie waited.

"I've decided not to see Adriana again until after our annulment comes through."

Cassie looked at him in surprise. "Why?"

"Because that's the way it should be. It was inexcusable that you were subjected to the humiliation of showing up at my apartment to find my mistress acting as my hostess."

"But that wasn't your fault...."

"It shouldn't have happened, Cassie. It doesn't matter that our vows were meaningless. You are legally my wife and as such you deserve my respect and consideration." His eyes rested on her lovely face. "I just wanted you to know that."

His gesture made Cassie feel warm and happy inside. "Thank you," she said quietly.

"You're welcome." Then he looked at his watch and got to his feet, pulling Cassie up with him. His finger trailed a gentle path under her eye. "Get some sleep," he said softly. "You've had a long day, and I'm a little tired myself."

His touch sent a shiver of awareness through her and she moved slightly out of his reach. "Good night."

"Good night, Cassie." He opened the door for her and quietly closed it after her.

She stood there thoughtfully for a long moment before turning out the light and curling up on a chair near the window. She was tired, but she didn't really want to go to sleep yet. It was very quiet. A cool night breeze gently lifted the curtains and washed over her. She heard movement in Franco's room, and then his light went out. She assumed he had gone to bed—until she heard his door open and close a few minutes later.

Then she heard the closing of another door, this one outside, below her window, and she leaned forward in the darkness to see. Franco moved into her line of vision and then stopped. He lit a cigarette. A moment later another man stepped from the shadows into the moonlight. He was a big fellow, almost as tall as Franco, but with a broader build. A rifle hung casually by a strap over his shoulder. The two of them talked in low voices for several minutes and then moved off together, away from the house.

Cassie leaned back in her chair. What on earth was going on?

Chapter Three

The next morning Cassie woke early. After she had dressed she paused in front of the door connecting her room to Franco's. Her hand hovered over the knob, but then she pulled it back. Whether or not he had come back last night was none of her business.

Instead, she walked down the hall to Sam's room and quietly opened the door. The rumpled bed was empty. The clothes he had worn the day before lay in a heap in the middle of the floor. Cassie shook her head and smiled as she picked them up and folded them neatly. Sam was Sam. Keeping his room straight had never been high on his list of priorities.

Still smiling, Cassie went downstairs with a light step, ready to enjoy her first day in Italy.

"Signora!"

Cassie turned to find Maria following her. "Good morning."

Maria smiled. "Come. I'll take you to breakfast."

Cassie followed her into the warm Italian sunshine. A round table on the lawn had been laid with a white cloth and china, but Cassie hardly noticed. It was Franco, already seated and reading a newspaper, who drew her attention. Maria went back into the house as Cassie walked across the lawn to the table and quietly seated herself. Franco lowered his paper. "Good morning, Cassie."

"Good morning."

"Were you finally able to sleep last night?"

"After awhile."

He went back to reading his newspaper and Cassie had to smile. So this was what marriage was like.

Maria brought out some croissants and fresh coffee and Franco folded his paper and laid it next to his plate. "Have you any plans for today?" he asked as he poured her a cup and then one for himself.

"Nothing specific. I thought I'd wander through your villa and get to know it, since I'll be living here. Is that all right?"

"Of course. Make yourself at home. And if you want to go horseback riding, there is a stable beyond the olive grove. I'll tell the man in charge to let you have whatever horse you like."

Cassie was surprised and just a little hurt at how impersonal he sounded this morning after their conversation last night. She had expected him to be a little more friendly. "Thank you."

"I don't want you going in to Rome alone, though. Stay on the grounds."

"Why?"

He lifted a dark brow. "Because I said so."

Cassie wasn't used to being spoken to as though she were a child, and she didn't like it. "That answer hasn't worked with me since I was ten."

A corner of his carved mouth lifted. "I'm sorry, Cassie. I should have said that I prefer that you stay here unless I—or someone I trust—go with you."

"Why?"

"Because of the problems I spoke of yesterday. It was your decision to stay in Italy. The result of that decision is that there are going to be some house rules for you to follow."

"All right." Not realizing that she was staring at him rather rudely, Cassie studied him, a small frown creasing her forehead.

Franco looked at her over the rim of his cup. "Why are you looking at me like that?"

"You're very different from any man I've ever met before."

"And what kind of men do you usually meet?"

"American men, I suppose. Over the past two decades American men have gone through a lot of changes. They show their feelings, express tenderness. Some of them even cry."

"This isn't America."

"Believe me, no one is more aware of that than I. But just from my short time at your dinner party last night, I noticed that you're not like other Italian men, either."

He seemed genuinely interested in her amateur analysis, and just a little amused. "And how do I differ from other Italian men?"

"You're quieter. You don't wear your emotions on your sleeve. It's very difficult to tell what you're thinking or what your reactions are."

He took another sip of coffee and leaned back in his chair, his eyes on her. "So I'm not like ordinary American men and I'm not like ordinary Italian men. What does that make me?"

Cassie thought about it for a moment. "No ordinary man," she finally said. "You're not like anyone else."

His eyes met hers for a long moment. "Nor are you, Cassandra Luciano. Nor are you."

Cassie's heart began a rhythmic pounding beneath her breast. Had it been doing that all along without her noticing it, or had it just started because of the way he was looking at her?

Franco glanced at his watch, then tossed his napkin on the table. "I have an early court appearance in Rome this morning. I'll be back tonight."

"All right."

"If you need anything or have any questions, Taddeo will be here. If you go out riding, take Enzo with you."

"Enzo?"

"You'll meet him today." He rose, but hesitated. It was as if he were reluctant to leave her.

"I'll be fine. Really," Cassie said.

Franco inclined his dark head and was gone. Cassie's eyes followed him into the villa. She liked looking at him, and it wasn't just because he was handsome. It went deeper than that. He radiated power—physical power. Cassie was drawn to him, and it worried her a little. He wasn't the kind of man to whom she had pictured herself being attracted. She liked men who were gentle and easy to read. Uncomplicated. All she needed to round out a really disastrous year was to fall in love with the wrong man, she thought wryly.

"Hey, Cassie!"

She came back to her surroundings with a start and turned to find Sam running across the lawn toward her with two dark-haired boys of about his own age, a woman bringing up the rear. "Hi." Cassie smiled, ruffling her brother's hair when he came to a panting stop beside her chair. "What have you been up to?"

The other two boys caught up and stood next to Sam, their dark eyes dancing. "Cassie," Sam introduced, "these are my two new friends, Gino and Tony."

She smiled at them as well. "How do you do?"

They grew suddenly shy. The woman finally caught up and collapsed, laughing, into the chair Franco had just vacated. "These two—" she inclined her head toward Gino and Tony between breaths "—belong to me. I'm Diane Juliano. We're neighbors."

Cassie shook the fair-haired Englishwoman's hand. "Hello. I'm Cassie Wilde...uh, Luciano."

Diane studied her curiously. "Sam told me that you're married to Franco. I was surprised to hear it."

"So was everyone else."

"How did the two of you meet?"

"Oh, the usual, boring way," Cassie said, sidestepping.

Diane took the hint and changed the subject. "I hope you don't mind, but my children seem to spend most of their time here. And now that Sam will be living in the villa, they'll probably become glued to this place.''

Cassie smiled. ''That's not a problem. They're more than welcome. I'm glad there's someone for Sam to play with.''

Gino tugged at his mother's blouse, and Diane smiled and patted his hand. ''I almost forgot what I came for. My boys were wondering if Sam could spend the day with us.''

Cassie hesitated, but one glance at Sam's pleading face and she couldn't say no. ''I don't see why not—as long as he behaves and does what he's told,'' she added meaningfully.

Sam hugged her. ''I will! Thanks!'' And he and the two boys ran off.

Diane shook her head as she watched them disappear into the distance. ''Ah, to be a child again. It never ceases to amaze me how quickly they make friends.'' Then she turned back to Cassie. ''It's going to be a real pleasure having a neighbor whose first language is English. I hope we'll be seeing a lot of one another.''

''If your sons and my brother have anything to say about it, I'm sure we will.''

Diane laughed and went off after the boys.

Cassie dabbed at her mouth with her napkin, then set it neatly next to her plate and went back into the villa. Taddeo, coming out just as she was going in, nearly ran into her. He put his hands on her shoulders to steady her. ''Well, good morning.''

''Thank you.'' She smiled warmly. ''And good morning to you.''

''Where are you off to in such a hurry?''

"I thought I'd look around the villa. So far I've only seen my bedroom and the kitchen."

"Would you like a guide?"

"Are you volunteering?"

He clicked his heels together and gallantly held out his arm. "At your service, my lady."

Cassie placed her hand on his arm and forced an appropriately ladylike expression to her face. "Thank you. Where should we start?"

"With the main living quarters, I suppose. It's really quite a spectacular place."

It certainly was. The villa had everything: a music room with a beautiful grand piano; a library; a game room; a ballroom; an enormous living room with floor-to-ceiling doors that led to a courtyard; the whole villa was beautiful, yet somehow sterile. Beauty without warmth.

"Do you live here?" she asked.

"No. I spend most of my time in New York. I'm only here a few times a year."

"What do you do in New York?"

He glanced down at her. "Is that your subtle way of asking me if I have a job?"

"Apparently not, if you figured it out so easily."

Taddeo laughed and patted the hand she rested on his arm. "Well, in answer to your not-so-subtle question, I don't. I'm quite content to live off my inheritance." He glanced down at his companion and gave a theatrically heartfelt sigh. "And now I suppose you've lost all respect for me."

Cassie smiled. "I don't know you well enough to lose respect. Why do you live in New York and not Rome?"

He shrugged. "I suppose because I find New York more exciting. Something is always going on. Rome is too steeped in its ancient history for my taste. There's nothing new about it."

Cassie studied his downcast profile. There was obviously a lot more to his decision than that. "And?" she prodded.

Taddeo looked down at her and grinned as they walked. "You're awfully nosy."

"I know," she agreed amiably, and waited for him to elaborate.

"To be completely honest," he finally said, "it's a little hard following in my big brother's footsteps, and I'm tired of trying."

"Do you mean that he expects too much of you?"

Taddeo shook his head. "No, not Franco. He's one of the few people who accepts me just as I am. It's the other people in Roman society who can't resist comparing me and my nonexistent list of accomplishments with Franco's painfully long list. It's easier to live in New York where most people have never heard the name Luciano, and could probably not care less if they had." He studied Cassie's profile as they walked. "Perhaps after you and my brother part company we could get together. Illinois isn't all that far from New York. And something tells me I'm much more your type than Franco is."

"I'd like that," Cassie said after a moment. "I'd like that very much."

He glanced at his watch and his eyes widened. "I've really enjoyed this, Cassie, but unfortunately I have to be going. I'm already late for a date. See you tomorrow."

"Tomorrow? Won't you be home for dinner?"

"Not if my luck with women is holding out. I met someone last night...." He rolled his eyes heavenward and kissed his fingertips, then left.

"Signora." A gruff voice cut through the silence.

Cassie jumped and turned. The same man she had seen with Franco the night before stood a few feet behind her. She put her hand over her pounding heart. "Who are you?"

"Enzo," he said unsmilingly. "Signor Luciano asked me to look after you."

Somehow he sounded as thrilled about the deal as Cassie felt. "I see."

"Is there anything I can show you? Anything you need?"

"No, thank you."

He inclined his head and left. Cassie's curious eyes followed him. What a strange man.

Just then the maid walked by. "Maria?"

She came back and looked in the doorway. "Signora?"

"Who is the man who was just in here?"

"Why, that's Enzo."

"I know what his name is, but who is he? What does he do around here?"

"Many things. Sometimes he's a bodyguard. He runs errands for your husband occasionally, but never speaks of them." She lifted her shoulders. "He doesn't associate with the rest of the staff. I'm afraid we know little about him."

Cassie was disappointed. The man had piqued her curiosity. "Thank you." The maid bobbed her head and left, and Cassie went to her room to get her sketch pad and some pencils. She put them in an oversize shoulder bag, then went for a walk on the grounds. Grass paths wound through the garden. She followed first one and then another, amazed at how much area the gardens actually covered. One of the paths she took led her out of the garden and straight to the ruin of what had once been a villa. It was impossible to tell how old it was, but her amateur's guess was several hundred years. Broken statuary lay scattered on the dirt of what was once a floor. Faded tiles half covered the only standing wall, and weathered marble pillars towered sadly over the scene. One of the pillars had toppled over and lay on the earth in broken, round pieces. She sat on one of the sections and pulled out her sketch pad. With quick, neat lines, she captured the scene. Who had lived here all those centuries ago? she wondered.

As the sun set, her drawing grew more and more detailed, her artist's eye missing nothing. She even sketched in, with a light pencil, the ghostly figures of the Romans whose villa she imagined this was.

It was almost dark when she finally started back home. When the villa came into view she was surprised to see lights blazing from nearly every window. The inner courtyard was also flooded with light.

Her heart sank. Unless she was sadly mistaken, they were looking for her. She should have told someone where she was going, but she hadn't intended to be gone so long. Gearing up for the worst, she took a deep breath and went in through the living-room doors. Several men were in the room, but Cassie's eyes went straight to Franco and, as though he sensed her presence, he turned. She could have sworn she saw relief flash across his face, but then his jaw tightened as he strode over to her. The other men in the room grew absolutely silent as Franco took her none too gently by the arm and led her to his library, closing the door behind them. "Where in the hell have you been?"

"Sketching," she offered lamely. "I forgot about the time."

"You also forgot to tell anyone where you were going. I was just about to send some men out to look for you."

"I'm sorry."

Franco ran his fingers through his dark hair. "Cassie," he said, his voice quiet, "we thought something had happened to you."

"I've said I'm sorry, but I think you're carrying this protectiveness of yours a little too far. I was on the grounds."

"Alone." He paced back and forth for a moment and then came to a stop in front of her. "I've given this more thought."

Cassie knew what was coming. "And you want me to go to Switzerland."

"No. The more I think about it, the more I think I can protect you better here, but only if you do as you're told. You must take Enzo with you whenever you plan on wandering far from the villa. I know it's inconvenient, but I wouldn't ask you if I didn't think it was necessary."

Cassie started to argue, but caught herself and closed her mouth. She had no intention of taking that man with her wherever she went, but there was no point in making an issue of it. That was an argument she could never win.

"I've also been thinking about Sam." He walked away from her and went to stand by the doors leading to the courtyard.

Cassie was suddenly alert. "What about Sam?"

"He isn't in the house right now. Do you know where he is?"

"At Diane Juliano's."

He nodded his dark head. "Good. They're nice people."

"What about Sam?" Cassie repeated.

Franco turned back to her. "I'd like him to go to boarding school with Gino and Anthony. I mentioned it to him this morning and he seemed to like the idea."

Cassie shook her head. "No. Absolutely not. The whole reason we're here is so that Sam can stay with me. If he's going to be in boarding school, he might as well be living with Aunt Emily."

"That's not true, Cassie. Besides, it won't be for long. Just until the judge signs the custody papers. Then both of you can go back to America."

A frown of concern creased Cassie's forehead. "Do you really think Sam could be in some kind of danger because of your work?" she asked quietly.

Franco cupped her chin in his hand. "I think that you are far more vulnerable than your brother. But in boarding school he will be looked after constantly. That makes him a much less attractive target for someone seeking revenge on me."

Cassie still wasn't convinced.

"He will come home every weekend with Gino and Anthony," Franco coaxed.

"How long will this trial take?"

Franco lifted his shoulders. "It could be weeks. It could be months. Two of our most important witnesses have dropped out of sight in the last several days."

A chill wound its way through Cassie. "Do you think they're dead?" she asked quietly.

"Probably."

She had read countless stories in American newspapers about Italian judges and prosecutors, and even newsmen, being murdered because they were doing their jobs. Her thoughts were reflected on her expressive face.

Franco looked at her with surprising tenderness. "Do you always worry about people you hardly know?"

Cassie lowered her eyes and didn't answer, but Franco would have none of that, forcing her eyes back to his.

"What are you thinking?"

"That I like you very much," she answered quietly. "And that I don't want to see anything happen to you." She shook her head and moved away from him. "Why are you involved in this kind of work at all?"

"Someone has to do it."

"But why you?"

"Do you hear yourself, Cassie? If everyone thought that way, criminals would never be prosecuted."

"I don't like it." Suddenly a corner of her mouth lifted and she looked up at Franco. "I'm sounding very wifely, aren't I?"

He smiled back at her, charmed by her sudden change of direction. The emotional chemistry between them filled the room.

There was a quick knock on the door. "Come," Franco called.

Enzo entered and looked directly at Franco without even acknowledging Cassie's presence. Charming man. "Your clerk is here."

"I'll just be a moment longer."

Enzo gave a small bow and left, and Franco looked back at Cassie. "I have a lot of work to catch up on tonight."

"Of course." Cassie started for the door, but turned before she reached it. "Will I see you at dinner?"

Franco had already moved behind his desk to pick up a file. He raised his head at her question. "No. I'm having something brought in here."

Their eyes locked for a long moment. "I'll see you in the morning, then."

"Good night, Cassie."

"Good night."

As she left the library, a young man carrying an armload of files hurried past her and closed the door behind himself with his foot.

As she started up the stairs, the doorbell chimed. Cassie went to open it and found Sam standing there with his two new friends and Diane. "Hi, Cassie," he called as he raced past her and up the stairs with Gino and Tony.

Diane shook her head. "They've been running all day. I'm exhausted just from watching."

Cassie laughed and stepped aside for the woman to enter. "It was nice of you to take him for the day. He obviously enjoyed himself."

"I think so. I know my two had a wonderful time."

"Can you stay for a few minutes and have a glass of wine with me while Sam shows the boys his room?"

Diane glanced at her watch. "Thank you. I'd like that. My husband won't be home for another hour."

Maria appeared and Cassie told her what they wanted. When she had gone Cassie led Diane into the living room. "What does your husband do?" she asked as they sat on the comfortable circular couch.

"He's an attorney in Franco's law firm. Didn't your husband tell you?"

"We haven't had much of a chance to talk since I got here yesterday."

Diane nodded sympathetically. "I understand, believe me. There are times when Paolo, my husband, has a case on his mind, and it's as though I don't exist for days at a time. The case is all he can think about." Then Diane smiled. "But as a newlywed I don't imagine Franco will start neglecting you for his work for at least a few months."

Cassie really liked Diane, and wanted to be honest with her. "There's something you should understand about my marriage to Franco. We aren't in love and we don't plan to stay married very long. He's simply helping me keep custody of Sam.'

Diane was genuinely surprised. There was something about the way Cassie looked whenever Franco's name was mentioned that told of anything but a marriage of convenience.

Maria brought them their wine and then left them alone. Diane leaned forward and clinked her glass against Cassie's. "Well, whatever the circumstances, it's nice to have you for a neighbor."

"Thanks. I feel the same way about you." Cassie sipped her wine. "How long have you known my husband?"

"For years. Since childhood, actually. My father was a British diplomat stationed in Rome. My parents were friends of Franco's parents."

"Where are his parents?" she asked curiously. "I've met his brother and heard about his grandmother, but he's never mentioned his parents."

Diane shook her head. "No, he wouldn't. They're both dead. You see, Franco's father was once a special government prosecutor, just as Franco is now. One day, when Franco was only ten, his mother was gunned down on a street in Rome, in retaliation for a guilty verdict found against an underworld criminal. Franco was with her, and he was badly hurt himself.

Quick tears stung Cassie's eyes. "Oh, no," she whispered.

"It was terrible. His father never recovered from the guilt he felt over being the cause of his wife's death. He committed suicide less than a year later. The whole thing left Franco with some very deep emotional scars that he won't admit to."

"How could it not?"

Diane nodded. "From that time on he was determined to take over where his father left off, but with a difference. No family. No ties to anyone other than Taddeo and their grandmother. He has his women, certainly, but he never allows himself to get seriously involved. I think it's because he doesn't ever want what happened to his mother to happen to a woman he loves."

"That makes sense."

"Unfortunately, that's true."

Diane watched Cassie's changing expressions with interest. "What are you thinking?" she finally asked.

Cassie's eyes returned to her guest. "That I wish he were in some other line of work. Don't you worry about your husband?"

Diane shook her head. "There's no need. He's not involved in the same cases as Franco. He handles small civil matters mostly, and he never does any work for the government." She got to her feet. "And speaking of my husband, I'd better be heading home—now that I've given you enough material for nightmares for years to come."

"Some friend you turned out to be," Cassie said dryly.

Diane smiled, but her tone was serious. "I'd like us to be friends, Cassie. And I hope that you'll keep what I've said to yourself. I just had a feeling that Franco wouldn't tell you. I've never known him to mention it."

"I won't say anything."

They walked into the foyer and Diane called up the stairs for her children. All three boys came racing down, and with a smile and a shake of her head, Diane led her two outside and headed for home. Cassie thoughtfully closed the door behind them.

"What's for dinner?" Sam asked, bringing her back to her surroundings.

She looked down at him and smiled. "I don't know. Are you hungry?"

"Starving. They sure eat late around here."

Cassie put her hand on his shoulder. "They sure do. Let's go to the kitchen to find out what's going on."

A few hours later dinner was finished, Sam was asleep in his bed and Cassie was sitting quietly in a chair by her bedroom window, reading a book. A breeze drifted in, lifting the curtains and gently touching her skin.

With a sigh, she raised her eyes from the mystery she was reading just in time to see a movement in the courtyard below. Cassie quickly turned out the light and knelt by her window, peering into the darkness. A shadow moved in the moonlight. It looked like the mysterious Enzo. With only a slight hesitation, Cassie pulled on jeans and a dark sweater and moved stealthily through the house to the front door and then outside. She didn't feel as though she were in any danger. After all, no one knew she was there. She was doing the stalking. She stood very still in the shadows, waiting and watching, until she saw another movement. A break in the clouds confirmed what she already knew. It was Enzo, walking with a small sack thrown over his shoulder. Her heart beat accelerated as she followed him, her footsteps silent on the dew-dampened grass. There was something about Enzo she didn't trust, and she wanted to find out what he was up to.

She stepped on a twig and it snapped. Cassie stood absolutely motionless and held her breath for a moment, wondering if Enzo had heard. But the man some twenty yards ahead of her kept moving, and she started up again, this time more careful about where she stepped. Perhaps a little too careful. Enzo was able to move a lot more quickly than she, and as a result, she lost him.

Cassie stopped in the middle of the olive grove and looked around. Her heart was pounding in her ears, and only now did it occur to her that she had been foolhardy in coming out here without telling anyone. It was one thing to be following someone; it was quite another to lose him and suddenly wonder if you were the one being followed. And to top it off, she was now completely lost. Her sense of direction had never been very strong, and at the moment she hadn't the faintest idea which direction was the way back to the villa.

She moved forward tentatively, then stopped and looked around. Clouds were once again blocking the moonlight, preventing her from seeing anything very clearly. She moved forward again, slowly, deliberately, until she came to the end of the grove. There, in the clearing, was a small cottage. Lights were on inside and she could make out some people in the living room. Enzo walked past a window and Cassie relaxed a little, now that she knew he was there and not behind her. But what was he up to?

She bent low and crept up to the cottage, her head just below the window. Slowly she raised herself until her eyes just peeped above the outer window ledge. To her amazement, Franco was in the room, talking to a man she had never seen before, while the clerk she had passed earlier sat taking notes on what was being said. Enzo walked over to Franco and spoke quietly. A look of anger crossed Franco's face as he rose abruptly and started for the door. Cassie gasped, realizing that Enzo must have spotted her and told her husband. Completely forgetting about dignity, she straightened and raced back into the olive grove, climbing the nearest tree. Her impulsive curiosity had gotten her into some minor trouble before, but nothing like this. Enzo was obviously not up to anything more sinister than doing what he was told by his boss, and if Franco were to catch her out here like this, she'd feel like the fool she was.

Suddenly the limb on which she was perched creaked and sank a little lower, and so did Cassie's heart. She couldn't believe this was happening to her. She closed her eyes tightly and wished for the limb not to sink any lower, but it didn't help. It creaked and sank some more, and then finally snapped away from the tree altogether, with a noise that sounded like a shot, and sent her plummeting seven feet to the ground. The very solidly packed ground.

Cassie remained perfectly still for a long moment, winded but unharmed. When she opened her eyes it was to find Franco standing over her, unsmiling and unsympathetic.

Cassie smiled and weakly rippled her fingers at him. "Hi there. I can explain this...."

Chapter Four

Cassie raised herself onto her elbows, her eyes never wavering from the man towering above her. There was a sudden break in the clouds, and the moonlight illuminated Franco's face. The grooves in his cheeks were deep and the corner of his mouth twitched. Cassie's mouth parted softly. "You're laughing at me!"

His teeth flashed white in his dark face as he reached out a helping hand and pulled Cassie to her feet. "You'd laugh too if you could see how ridiculous you look. Are you injured?"

She brushed the dirt from her jeans while Franco moved behind her to brush the dirt and leaves from her sweater. "Only my dignity," she said dryly. She heard him laugh out loud for the first time. It was a rich, infectious sound that made Cassie smile, too.

With his hands on her shoulders, he turned her to face him and concentrated on picking the leaves out of her hair. "What in the hell are you doing climbing olive trees in the middle of the night?"

"Not to mention falling out of olive trees in the middle of the night."

"That, too."

"You're going to be angry."

"Probably."

She took a deep breath. "I was following Enzo. I saw the two of you taking off in the middle of the night yesterday, and tonight when I saw him skulking around the courtyard again I couldn't resist. I wanted to see what he was up to." She paused for a moment. "Nice evening, isn't it?"

"Don't change the subject. I told you when you first arrived here that you'd probably see some things you wouldn't understand and not to question them, yet here you are."

"I know. It's just that sometimes my curiosity gets the better of me."

"It also killed the cat. Remember that the next time you're tempted to do something idiotic."

Cassie flinched a little. "Yes, sir." Then she cleared her throat. "But since I'm already out here, and I went to all that trouble to make a fool of myself, would you mind telling me what's going on?"

Franco shook his head. "Cassie, you're incorrigible."

Her smile flashed. "I know. That's part of my charm."

"No, it isn't," he said dryly as he took her cold hand in his warm one and led her toward the cottage. Enzo waited outside, his face expressionless as he opened the door and closed it behind them. The same middle-aged man she had seen through the window rose nervously at their entrance, and his eyes kept going to the door, as though he were expecting trouble. Franco explained who she was and that no one had followed her, but the man still seemed to have trouble relaxing.

Suddenly Cassie understood. This man was a witness and Franco was hiding him on his property.

Her husband caught her eye and motioned his head toward the other end of the cottage. Cassie walked to a chair about ten feet behind Franco and sat quietly while he finished asking the man questions.

She was fascinated. Signor Salvatore had some incredible stories to tell of extortion and drug-running. Even murder. Franco listened impassively, interjecting questions to get clearer information. But to Cassie, the whole thing was so farfetched that it was like watching a movie. Things like this didn't really happen. It was pure Hollywood. For three hours she sat there and listened attentively. Some things she missed, because when the man got excited he spoke too quickly for her to follow. One name seemed to come up over and over again, though: Alessandro Forli.

Her eyes occasionally wandered to Enzo. He was in and out. He no longer seemed so sinister.

Finally Franco rose and shook Signor Salvatore's hand in parting, then put his arm around Cassie's shoulders and walked her outside. Enzo was standing by the door. Franco told him to stay there for the night, and the man wordlessly dipped his head and folded his arms across his chest.

As they walked through the olive grove, Cassie sensed Franco's need for silence. Every once in a while he would reach out a hand to help her over a high root or a rock, and whenever his hand touched her a wave of awareness would roll gently through her body. It surprised her, because she had never had that reaction to a man before, and she had never expected to experience it with a man as alien to her as Franco Luciano.

When they finally came out of the olive grove and into the courtyard Franco stopped and stood very still as he studied the dark sky. Cassie looked up also, until she felt his gaze on her profile. Her eyes met his as a cool breeze lifted the silky hair from the back of her neck. "What are you thinking, Cassandra Luciano?" he asked quietly.

She gazed at him steadily. "That none of this is real. That we're not really married, and there's no gangster staying at the cottage."

He reached out a warm hand and cupped her cheek as his eyes rested on her beautifully defined mouth. Without any warning he lowered his head and captured it with his. It was a kiss of devastating gentleness, a searching kiss, as though he were trying to get to know her; to get to know the taste of her. And though their bodies never touched and his arms never went around her to pull her closer, Cassie grew weak with the yearning he drew out of her. Franco lifted his head and gazed into her surprised blue eyes. His thumb gently rubbed the spot where his mouth had so recently been. "And that the kiss never really happened," he said softly. "Good night, Cassie." He walked away from her and into the villa.

Cassie sank onto the lawn chair behind her and placed her hand over her racing heart. What was happening to her? What was there about this man that could turn her knees to jelly?

She shook her head. Whatever it was she was going to have to get over it. If she were to fall in love with him, it would only lead to pain. There was no place in his life for her, and she had to remember that.

Besides, a kiss was just a kiss, not a declaration. It would be a mistake for her to read too much into what had just happened.

Cassie took a deep breath, slowly exhaled, then rose from the lawn chair and went to her room.

A hand vigorously shook her shoulder. Cassie blinked several times before she was able to focus. Franco stood over her bed. "Wake up!"

She blinked again, and then rubbed her eyes with the backs of her hands. "What are you doing here?"

"Trying to get you out of bed."

Cassie frowned at him and closed her eyes again before hugging her pillow to her and rolling onto her side. "Go away."

"Is this my charming Cassie?"

"I don't get charming until at least nine A.M." She reached over and picked up her watch from the night table, then opened one eye to glance at the dial. "That means I have another fifteen minutes to go," she informed the intruder as she put the watch back and curled up with her pillow again. "Now go away."

She felt the weight of his body sink the mattress as he sat on the edge of her bed, and then he was perfectly still. She managed to lie there for another sixty seconds and then she couldn't stand it any longer. With a huge sigh, she rolled onto her back and looked up at him. His hazel eyes roamed over her sleep-flushed cheeks and the dark hair that tumbled over her white pillow. With a gentle hand, he reached out and pushed a silky strand away from her face. What was there about this particular woman that was affecting him so deeply after knowing her such a short time? "It's Sunday. I thought you might like to go into Rome with me this morning to do some sightseeing."

Cassie was suddenly alert. "I would! I'd love to!" She raised herself up on her elbows, completely un-self-conscious about his being in her bedroom. "Have you talked to Sam yet?"

"He seems to think going to see the Roman Forum would be excruciatingly boring. He'd rather spend the day with Gino and Anthony. How soon can you be ready?"

Cassie threw back the covers and padded, bare-foot, across the floor to the armoire. "Five minutes," she told him over her shoulder as she grabbed some clothes and walked into the bathroom. Then she poked her head back around the door. "Are we really going to see the Roman Forum?"

"Really."

"And the Pantheon?"

"If you like."

"I'd like." The door clicked shut again. Franco smiled as he rose from the bed and left the room.

True to her word, Cassie was downstairs in five minutes, dressed in a full white skirt and a white short-sleeved blouse. Her dark hair was styled simply, brushed away from her face and held back with a narrow plastic band. Over one shoulder hung the strap of an extra-large purse that held her sketch pad and pencils. Franco came out of the library at the same moment as Cassie reached the bottom step. "Hi," she said with a smile.

Franco glanced at his watch in surprise and then back at her. "Hello."

"As you get to know me better, you'll find that I'm shockingly punctual."

"I'll look forward to it." He walked to the front door and held it open for her. Cassie stepped out into the bright new day and followed Franco to his black Ferrari. This was the first time she had had a good look at it. It was a beautiful car, and oddly suited to its owner. When he started the engine it was quiet and low, and it seemed to exude the same leashed power as Franco.

As they drove she gazed out at the passing scenery. It was late in the summer and the hot Italian sun had scorched the earth, leaving dried brown grass where once it had been green. The sky was a deep blue, with no clouds to speak of. The highway was a wide, modern one that cut through the ancient countryside, and the traffic was almost nonexistent. "Where are all the people?" she wondered aloud.

"It's a religious holiday. Many are at the Vatican listening to the Pope. Others are at home, watching him on television."

Several minutes passed. Cassie knew exactly when they entered the city because suddenly the buildings were so close together it would have been difficult to get a knife between them. The roads narrowed and traffic became a little heavier. "Cassie, look."

She turned her attention from the passenger window to the view through the windshield, and she gasped as the Colosseum suddenly loomed before them. Cassie had seen photographs of it, like everyone else, but she was still awed by its size and the magnificence of its architecture. She knew its history, and some of the awful things that had gone on within its walls, but it was still a beautiful piece of work.

Franco saw her rapt expression and smiled. "Do you realize that it took the Romans only a few years to build that? And with only manual labor. Now, with the bureaucracy we have, and a new government every year, it would take decades." They stopped at a red light, in full view of the ancient structure. "And across the street—and a little difficult to see from here—is the Forum. There are no cars allowed in there. It's strictly footpaths, but it's a nice walk."

She moved forward in her seat to stare at a remarkably well-preserved arch not far from the Forum. It was huge and graceful, full of history. "That's the Arch of Constantine, isn't it?" she asked softly.

Franco studied it and nodded. "It needs a little work. The air pollution is destroying the marble."

"It's magnificent. Your whole history is magnificent."

He glanced sideways at her. "It's your history, too, Cassie."

"Once removed," she smiled.

The light changed and they drove on, deeper into Rome, until they came to its heart, the Via Veneto. It was a charming, wide boulevard lined with grand old hotels, embassies and very expensive shops. What Cassie liked best about the street was that all the buildings had a comfortably worn look about them, perked up by the bright umbrellas of sidewalk cafés.

Franco pulled the car onto the sidewalk to park it, just as Taddeo had the night she had arrived. "Where are we going?" she asked, looking up at a two-story structure.

"My grandmother's apartment. She returned from Florence last night and asked to see you. I assumed you would have no objections."

"Of course not." Cassie stepped out of the car and smoothed her skirt. "Do I look all right?" she asked him.

His gaze warmed her. "You look lovely."

Cassie smoothed her skirt again anyway.

Franco placed a finger under her chin and raised her face to his. "There's no need to be nervous," he reassured her. "She's a perfectly nice lady."

"I know that," Cassie said softly. "But she's my godmother. She sent you to rescue me without ever having met me, and I owe her a lot. I want her to like me."

"Of course she'll like you. She'd have to be a fool not to, and my grandmother is nobody's fool."

Cassie took a deep breath and straightened her shoulders, then turned like a soldier marching off to war and walked into the building, oblivious to the amused glance of the man beside her. Their knock was answered by a young woman who grew visibly flustered at the sight of Franco. Before they could say anything, his grandmother walked into the foyer. She was a tall, handsome woman with white hair that was braided and wrapped around her head like a crown. And appropriately so: her bearing was completely regal. She kissed Franco on both cheeks and then walked over to Cassie and stood in front of her, taking both of her hands. "So you are dear Elena's child," she said softly. "And you look exactly as she did at your age. You even have her blue eyes."

There was something in her voice that aroused Cassie's curiosity. "Is there something wrong?"

"No, no, of course not," the older woman answered a little too quickly, causing Franco to narrow his eyes. She kissed Cassie on both cheeks and smiled. "This is a wonderful day for me. Come, child. Sit with me on the terrace and tell me about yourself." She pulled Cassie's arm through hers and strolled into the apartment and through some open doors to a terrace beyond. It was surrounded by flowers, some bright, some faded by the sun. But it was all charming. The noise of the city below somehow belonged. Franco joined them at a round, cloth-covered table, but didn't enter into the conversation. He seemed content to sit back and listen. But even so, Cassie was intensely aware of his presence.

"I understand you have a younger brother named Sam," she continued as the maid brought them glasses of lemonade. "How is he handling the changes in his life?"

Cassie smiled. "With a lot more élan than his sister, fortunately. He thinks he's on some kind of wonderful vacation. He's already making new friends."

"That's so nice."

Cassie studied her for a long moment. "How did you come to be my godmother? Mother never really talked about her life in Italy, so I know very little."

Signora Luciano smiled reminiscently. "Your mother, Elena, went to boarding school with my daughter. They were best friends. She spent many happy holidays with us. Right here, as a matter of fact, in this very apartment.''

"Not at the villa?''

"I never liked the villa. It's too secluded. I prefer the closeness of the city, and this is where we spent most of our time.''

"My mother must have been very fond of you.''

Signora Luciano nodded. "Elena was a delight and I loved her dearly. She was almost like a second daughter to me.''

"What about my mother's family? Do they live near here? I'd like to meet them if there's anyone left.''

Again the older woman seemed uneasy, and again Franco's eyes narrowed curiously on her. "I'm afraid they're all dead.''

Cassie was disappointed. "That's too bad. She never spoke of her parents, so I really don't know anything about them.''

"I wish I could help you in that regard, but I'm afraid I didn't know them very well.'' Signora Luciano seemed anxious to change the subject. "Franco tells me that you're an artist. Your mother was very talented. I've kept many of the pictures she sketched and painted during her visits. If you'd like to see them sometime, I'd love to show them to you. She had a wonderful talent.''

"Yes, she did,'' Cassie agreed quietly.

The signora reached across the table and clasped one of Cassie's hands in her own. "You are very much like her. And I must admit I feel as though I know you even though we just met. Your mother was an avid letter writer, and through her loving eyes I watched you grow up.''

"I didn't know that. She rarely spoke of you, and never showed me any letters you might have written her." Cassie hesitated for a moment, trying to find the right words to ask her next question. "There's something I haven't quite figured out, signora. How did you find out about my personal problems? No one knew but my attorney and myself."

Signora Luciano smiled and leaned back in her chair. "I hope you won't be offended, but I had Franco use his resources to check on you once or twice a year after your mother's death, just to make sure everything was all right. When your father died, Franco's sources got wind of the debt with which he had saddled you which, I'm sorry to say, didn't surprise me in the least. That's when I asked him to intervene. Just attribute it to a pushy old age." She glanced at her grandson. "But even so, I never expected him to marry you."

Cassie's eyes met Franco's. "I would have lost Sam if he hadn't."

The older woman nodded as she looked from one to the other. "Ahh. I see. There's nothing personal involved."

Cassie's eyes were still locked with her husband's. "That's right. Nothing personal."

Signora Luciano wasn't very happy about what she was seeing. She had done what she felt she should to help her goddaughter, but never in her wildest imaginings had she expected Franco to marry the girl. If her real background—one Cassie didn't know about—

were to become public knowledge, Franco's career could be ruined.

But still, she was very likable. It was a shame, really. "What are you two planning for the day?"

Cassie tore her eyes away from Franco. Her heart had started its now familiar racing beneath her breast. "Sightseeing."

Signora Luciano nodded. "This is a good day for it. The locals are celebrating their holiday and the tourist season is almost over. You should find yourselves nearly alone."

Franco glanced at his watch and rose. "If you'll excuse us, Grandmother, I think we should be going. We have a lot to see."

He helped Cassie to her feet and then bent low to kiss his grandmother's cheek. "I'll talk to you later."

She smiled affectionately at him and then at Cassie. "Good-bye, darlings. Have a lovely day."

When they went downstairs and were sitting in the car, Franco glanced at Cassie. "Now that wasn't too bad, was it?"

Cassie smiled at him, and his heart caught at the charm of it. "No, it wasn't," she said simply.

"She's a good woman," he told her as he put the Ferrari into gear and headed for the Forum. He parked on the road and then they walked to the main entrance of the Forum, not a hundred yards from the Colosseum. "This was the Basilica Emilia," Franco explained as they descended into the archaeological complex.

Cassie looked at him in confusion. "Basilica?"

"Back in the second century B.C. the word *basilica* referred not to a church, but to a particular architectural form developed by the Romans, a great hall that served as a court of law or a center for business and commerce. Many of them were later converted into Christian churches." He took Cassie's hand and led her over the rocky paths beyond the Basilica Emilia.

"What's that?"

Franco's gaze followed her pointing finger to a large brick Curia. "That's where the Roman Senate met in the late third century A.D. The open space in front is called the Comitium, which was the political center of ancient Rome. It was from there that Mark Antony delivered his funeral address to Julius Caesar's honor."

Cassie's sense of history almost overwhelmed her. She was standing where Mark Antony and Julius Caesar had once stood. Where countless Roman emperors had stood. Franco watched her rapt profile and smiled. He knew exactly how she felt. Not everyone had the imagination to appreciate something this awe-inspiring.

He showed her everything. The Forum proper, center of civic and social activity in ancient Rome; the countless temples where various sacred ceremonies were performed; and last, but far from least, the Arch of Titus, erected in A.D. 81 to celebrate the capture of Jerusalem ten years earlier.

Cassie stood before the arch and shook her head. "I want to do some sketches, but I don't know where to start."

Franco had played here as a child. Few knew the place as well as he did, and he took her to where he thought she'd have the best view of the Forum overall, the Temple of Vesta. Cassie sat on a fallen wall and pulled out her sketch pad and pencils and began capturing her surroundings with quick, efficient strokes. Franco sat on the wall several feet away from her, leaning against a half-fallen pillar and studying her profile as she worked. Her concentration was complete.

It was a whisper-quiet Sunday. The heat from the sun was intense, but somehow not uncomfortable. Insects buzzed lazily. The cats that were now the only inhabitants of the ancient Forum wandered with slow grace through the ruins. Suddenly a group of teen-aged tourists interrupted the peace with big radios raised high on their shoulders, blasting American rock music. It was so incongruous that Cassie turned with a smile to Franco. His eyes met hers in a long look, and a slow, answering smile curved his mouth. Then he closed his eyes and leaned the back of his head against the pillar, his face raised to the sun. He literally willed the tension to drain from his body. He couldn't remember the last time he'd had a genuinely relaxing day.

Cassie turned the page in her sketchbook and switched her attention from the ruins to the man sitting so nearby. Franco was an artist's dream. His face was more than handsome. It had character, with features that were straight and strong. She drew the corded muscles of his neck and the broad shoulders, and the muscular forearms, with the sleeves of his summer-white sweater pushed halfway up. The more she drew, the more she felt her attraction for the man growing. As she sketched his carved mouth, she found herself remembering how it had felt against hers the evening before, and suddenly she stopped drawing and just looked her fill. As though he felt her gaze, Franco opened his eyes and looked straight into hers. The teenagers were gone. The ruins were once again deserted, but for the two of them. His eyes caressed her lovely face. "Perhaps today was a mistake," he said quietly.

"Why?"

"Because I think I could get used to having you around, given the chance."

A delicious warmth filled Cassie as she realized that she had been thinking the same thing about him. There was a long silence between them. "Would that be such an awful thing?"

"Not awful, Cassie, but impractical. You might be half-Italian by blood, but you're all-American by nature. My world is completely different from yours."

"I can adapt."

"You shouldn't have to. What you need to do is find some nice American who lives a safe and comfortable life. I don't ever want anything to happen to you." He got to his feet and pulled Cassie to hers. "Are you hungry?"

She was disappointed at the change in subject, but went along with it. "Very."

"Let's get some lunch, then."

Cassie gathered her things and put them in her purse as they walked to his car. A few minutes later they had parked it near the Pantheon, the best-preserved monument of Imperial Rome. The piazza in front of the Pantheon was busier than the Forum. A woman stood on the edge of a fountain playing the violin, accompanied by a cassette of rich classical piano music. People gathered around her and listened in rapt attention, applauding when she finished and tossing coins into her open violin case. An outdoor café, set up so that its white-clothed tables faced the fountain and just beyond that, the Pantheon, was doing a brisk business. Waiters dressed in black trousers, starched white jackets and black ties moved gracefully and efficiently between the tables, delivering bottles of wine and plates of fragrant Italian pasta. As Cassie would discover, the waiters in Italy took great pride in their profession—because that was exactly what it was to them, a profession.

Cassie turned her attention back to the Pantheon. Huge monolithic columns and the original ancient bronze doors dating from 27 B.C. led into a truly magnificent room covered by a massive dome. Cassie looked straight up in wonder.

Franco followed her gaze. "This is the largest dome of its kind ever built. Its panels were once covered with gold, but that has been plundered over the centuries." He showed her the tombs of Raphael and two of Italy's monarchs.

Back out in the warm sunlight, Franco led her to an empty table at the café and they sat facing the Pantheon. "What are you thinking?" he asked as she sat staring at it.

"That the Italians have some remarkable engineers in their history. Imagine building something like that without the machinery we have to help us today, and doing it so well that it's lasted for nearly two thousand years."

A waiter came by and handed Franco a wine list. He glanced at it for just a moment and ordered. Cassie noticed that he looked, one by one, at the people at all the tables, and studied anyone new who happened by. He might seem calm and relaxed to the casual observer, but Cassie realized just how alert he was.

The waiter returned with the wine and opened it with a flourish at the table. It was rich, red and full of flavor. Franco ordered their lunch while Cassie broke some bread from a loaf in the bread basket and tossed some crumbs onto the pavement. Pigeons swooped from the skies and pecked it up and then waddled hopefully around their table, waiting for more, which Cassie obligingly gave them. Franco grinned as he watched her. "The waiters are going to love you for this."

Her smiling eyes met his. "They'll fly off as soon as someone walks through, but they're kind of fun to watch, don't you think?"

His hazel eyes focused on something over her head and his expression grew serious. Cassie straightened and turned to see what he was looking at. A tall, slender man in his seventies was being seated at a table about fifteen feet away. He had been looking at Franco, but his gaze moved to Cassie. Suddenly the half smile he had been wearing disappeared and his tanned face grew surprisingly pale as his eyes remained riveted on her. She found his reaction disconcerting. "Who is that?" she asked, turning back to Franco.

Franco, too, was a little surprised by the man's reaction to the sight of Cassie. "Alessandro Forli."

"Alessandro Forli," she said thoughtfully. "Isn't that the man your witness kept mentioning?"

"That's right."

"Well, who is he in relation to your witness?"

"An enemy."

Cassie looked at him in quiet disbelief. "Are you trying to tell me that that nice old man over there is some kind of criminal?"

"Not 'some kind,' Cassie. A very definite kind. He heads one of the largest crime families in Italy."

Cassie knew better than to turn her head to stare, but she was tempted. "But he doesn't look like a gangster."

A corner of Franco's mouth lifted at her naiveté. "And exactly what does a gangster look like?"

"More threatening. Less handsome."

"You've been watching too many American movies. Gangsters come in all kinds of packages. Though, I must admit, he's the last of a dying breed. A gentleman criminal. A man of his word despite his occupation."

Cassie studied her husband, a small smile playing at the corners of her mouth. "It sounds to me as though you actually respect this Forli fellow."

"It's one of his men I'm prosecuting right now."

"Genco?"

"That's right." He studied Alessandro Forli for a long time, seeming to forget Cassie was there. "I meant to tell you earlier that I'll be leaving town tonight and will be gone for about a week," he suddenly told her.

Cassie tried to hide her disappointment. She was going to miss him. "Where are you going?"

He brought his eyes back to her face and lightly touched her nose with his finger. "It won't do you any good to know that. I'll just tell you that it's on business."

"But..."

Franco shook his head, and a smile touched his eyes. "You ask more questions than any woman I've ever met."

Cassie closed her mouth over the question bubbling inside her.

The waiter brought their food, a timely interruption of their conversation. The pasta was delicious and Cassie savored every bite. When they finished eating a short time later, Franco paid the waiter, then put his hand under Cassie's elbow and helped her to her feet.

As they passed Alessandro Forli's table, the man inclined his head toward Franco, but his eyes were on Cassie, and she felt them on her back until they rounded a corner. Why was he so interested in her?

Franco seemed to sense her thoughts as he opened the car door for her. "It's because of your black hair and blue eyes. It's an unusual and beautiful combination."

"Thank you, but I don't think that's the reason."

He closed her door and then walked around the car and climbed into his seat. His eyes stared straight ahead as he started the engine. "Neither do I." And with that he slammed the Ferrari into gear and shot off into the traffic.

Chapter Five

A week later Cassie was in the garden, cutting flowers and arranging them in a basket. It was mostly for herself, because she hadn't seen Franco since the day they'd spent in Rome. She had been trying to brighten the villa a little, adding some warmth to its beauty.

Sam came outside, dressed in his new school uniform of dark blue slacks, white shirt and tie. The sight melted her heart, but she didn't hug him. Since coming to Italy, he'd become very independent and didn't want his sister babying him. It was a little hard for Cassie, but she was learning.

"Are you all packed?" she asked as she snipped the last flower and placed it in the basket.

He nodded. "Enzo should be here with Gino and Tony in a few minutes."

"Are you sure you don't want me to go with you? It's your first day...."

"You already went there with me once. I don't want the other boys to laugh at me."

"All right."

Enzo stood in the doorway and looked out at them. "The other boys are in the car. We should be leaving."

Cassie clasped her hands in front of her as she smiled down at her brother. "Good-bye. I'll see you Friday afternoon when you come home."

"'Bye, Cassie." She knew he was excited about going to boarding school. He'd danced around his room with Gino and Tony for five minutes when she'd told him he could. But now there was a little hesitation as he walked toward Enzo. Suddenly he turned and ran back to Cassie. She hunkered down and caught him in her arms.

"Oh, I'm going to miss you," she said softly.

Sam gave her one last squeeze and then grinned at her. "See you Friday." Then he ran off.

Taddeo came out of the house just then with a large package, beautifully wrapped. He raised it higher as Sam dashed under it and smiled after the boy. "I like that kid," he told her as he put the package on a nearby table, then walked over to Cassie and held out his hand to help her to her feet. "Don't look so sad, sister Cassie. He'll be back before you know it."

Cassie gave him a halfhearted smile.

"And over here," he said, leading her by the hand to the table, "is something that should cheer you up. A wedding present. And a heavy one, at that."

"You didn't have to do that."

"I didn't. I'm just the delivery boy. Someone dropped it off."

Cassie fingered the beautiful wrapping paper curiously. "I wonder who would be sending me a wedding present."

"Maybe there's a card inside. Open it."

She gently removed the paper and then lifted the lid of the large box. Inside was an elegant frame, perfect for a large wedding picture. Taddeo's whistle was long and low as he lifted it carefully from the box for a better look. "This is real gold, Cassie. It must have set the sender back a pretty penny."

Cassie touched the cool metal. "It's really beautiful."

Taddeo lowered it back into the box, then plucked a card out of the corner and read it aloud. "'Mrs. Luciano—May your marriage be a long and happy one. Alessandro Forli.'" He pursed his lips. "I'm impressed, Cassie."

"And I'm surprised. Why would he be sending me a wedding present?" she asked. "We haven't even met."

"Maybe he sends presents to all special prosecutors' new wives."

"Somehow I don't think so."

He gestured toward the gift. "So, what are you going to do with it?"

Cassie put the lid back on the box. "Return it to Signor Forli. I can't accept gifts from him or anyone else for a false marriage."

Taddeo clicked his tongue and lifted the lid slightly to gaze at the frame. "It's too bad, really. I could live for a year on the money that cost him." With a sigh, he dropped the lid back down and turned to kiss Cassie on the cheek. "I have a heavy date this afternoon."

Cassie's dimple flashed. "Do you have any idea how American you sound?"

"I should. I've lived there long enough." He took the car keys out of his pocket, tossed them into the air and caught them. "Good-bye, beautiful. Maybe I'll see you later, and maybe I won't."

Still smiling, Cassie went into the kitchen for a large vase and brought it outside, where she arranged the flowers in it. Maria came out to bring her some lemonade and started back into the villa, but Cassie stopped her. "Maria, is there a car around here I could borrow?"

"Yes, of course. Signor Luciano keeps several."

"Do you have the keys?"

"I know where they are."

"Would you please get me a set?"

Maria nodded and left. Cassie carried the flowers inside and set them on a table in the foyer. Then she went into the study and sat behind Franco's desk as she dialed the operator and asked for Alessandro Forli's telephone number. A few moments later his line was ringing. A woman answered, and then Signor Forli himself came on the line. Cassie was a little nervous. Franco would have her head on a platter if he knew what she was about to do, but her curiosity about the man wouldn't be stilled. "Signor Forli, this is Cassandra Luciano."

There was a small pause at the other end of the line. "Yes, Mrs. Luciano," he said, his English very good. "What may I do for you?"

"Well, I'd like to thank you for the beautiful wedding present."

"But...?"

"But I can't accept. I have to return it."

"I see."

"Could you please tell me where you live?"

"I can send a driver for it, if you'd like."

She knew that that was the way she should handle it, but she just couldn't let this opportunity slip by. "I'd rather return it myself, if that's convenient."

"Of course. My villa is fairly easy to find." He gave her directions that she copied onto a sheet of paper.

"Thank you. I'll see you shortly."

As soon as she'd hung up, Maria returned with a set of car keys. "This is to the red Fiat."

Cassie folded the paper with the directions and stuffed it into the pocket of her full pink skirt, then took the keys. "Thank you."

Maria hesitated. "Don't you think you should wait for Enzo to return? He's supposed to go with you whenever you leave the grounds."

"Not this time. I'm not going very far and I won't be in any danger."

An enormous frown still creased Maria's brow. Cassie brought out her mothering instincts.

"Oh, Maria." Cassie smiled at her and kissed her cheek. "Don't look so worried. I won't be gone long."

She went back into the courtyard for the frame, and a few minutes later, with the directions on the seat next to her and full of an anticipation she couldn't explain, she was on her way.

When she came to the driveway he'd mentioned she had to stop while a man came out of a small guard-house. "Would you please tell Signor Forli that Cassandra Wilde—uh, Luciano—is here to see him?"

Wordlessly, the man went back into the guard-house. She saw him speak into a telephone. A moment later the large gates that had been blocking the way swung open and she drove through and up the winding road to the villa. It was about the same size as Franco's, only much newer, and it had a pink cast to it, rather than dead white. A white-jacketed man opened the large, carved front door for her before she knocked, and he showed her through a wide hallway to an office.

Signor Forli rose from behind his desk at her entrance. "Signora Luciano, what a pleasant surprise." Again she noticed his fluent English. Then his eyes went to the package she held. "I'm sorry you decided not to accept the gift."

Cassie set it on his desk. "I really can't, but thank you. It's lovely."

"I thought so when I bought it. May I offer you some coffee or a cold drink?"

"Coffee would be nice, thank you."

He waved a hand at a man standing in the doorway, then motioned for Cassie to sit in a chair in front of his desk while he sat back in his. "I understand that you are recently arrived in Italy, signora."

"A little over a week ago." Now that she was here she wasn't a bit nervous. "And please, call me Cassie."

"Cassie," he repeated thoughtfully. "And that is a nickname for what?"

"Cassandra."

"And your maiden name is?"

"Wilde."

"I understand that your mother is Italian and your father American. What was your mother's maiden name?"

"Asti. Elena Asti. But my parents are both dead."

The man rose from his chair and walked over to a window, where he stood silently, looking outside. "When did they die?" he finally asked.

"My mother died about seven years ago, and my father just recently."

He was silent a little longer before finally turning back to her. A servant carried in a tray with coffee and cups on it and then left again, closing the study doors behind him. Signor Forli poured two cups and handed her one. Cassie noticed something puzzlingly familiar in many of his movements, and she found herself studying him with a curious eye. "Why did you seem so surprised to see me at the Pantheon?" she asked suddenly.

If she had expected to take him off guard, she was disappointed. He lifted his shoulders in a gentle shrug. "You bear a very strong resemblance to someone I once knew. For a moment I thought you were her." His eyes rested on her face. "I understand that you do some painting."

A smile touched Cassie's mouth. "You understand many things about me."

He smiled also. "I'll tell you why I'm bringing it up. For many years I've thought about having a portrait done of myself, but I've never taken the time to find a competent artist. Are you competent?"

"I'm more than competent. I'm good."

"A woman with confidence. I like that. And I'd like you to paint me."

She hesitated. Franco would never approve. "I'm expensive."

He lifted his shoulders. "You get what you pay for in life."

He certainly had an interesting face. She could imagine how extraordinarily handsome he had been when he was younger, because he was still a good-looking man at seventy. Besides, if she kept her eyes and ears open, she might just find out something that could help her husband. Cassie took the plunge. "I think I'd enjoy painting you."

He lifted his coffee cup to her. "When do we begin?"

"Whenever you'd like. Except for weekends."

"Of course. That is a time for families to be together." He thought for a moment. "I'm leaving tomorrow for several days, so how would it be if we began work on the portrait next Monday?"

"That sounds fine." She couldn't wait to get started. Cassie finished her coffee and rose. "I should leave now. I promised I wouldn't be gone long."

Signor Forli rose also and walked her to the study door. "I'm sorry you felt unable to accept my wedding gift, but I am glad the returning of it gave us an opportunity to meet."

"I am also."

The old man stood at the window of his study and watched her drive off. Another man, about his age, entered and stood next to his boss and friend. "Was that the girl of whom you spoke?"

Signor Forli nodded. "My granddaughter's name is Cassandra."

"She looks like Elena."

"They are identical."

"Did she tell you where Elena is?"

The old man was silent for a long moment, but it was obvious that he was going through an emotional struggle within himself. "My daughter is dead." He looked at his friend. "After she ran away all those years ago she changed her last name to Asti. That's why we couldn't find her." He stared back out the window. "Can you imagine being so ashamed of your father that you don't even want to carry his name?"

The other man's heart ached for his friend. He rested a comforting hand on his shoulder. "What's done is done, Alessandro. You can't change what is past. And Elena had no reason to be ashamed of you. You have done what you had to do over the years in order to survive."

"But how do you explain that to an idealistic teenager? I never could. And she never forgave me."

"But now you have another chance, with your granddaughter."

"No," he said firmly. "Cassandra must never find out who I am. I have an opportunity now to get to know her. To have her get to know me. But not as her grandfather." He smiled ironically. "Do you know who her husband is?"

"No."

"Franco Luciano."

The other man's eyes narrowed. He knew the name well. A sudden smile curved his lips. "So your granddaughter is married to the special prosecutor. You couldn't have planned things better."

The old man looked at his friend. "I will not have my granddaughter put in the middle of my war with her husband."

"But if word leaked out that he was married to *your* granddaughter, his credibility as a special prosecutor would be ruined, along with his career."

"No!" Alessandro slammed his fist down on his desk. "No one is to know of my relationship to Cassandra Luciano. And if anyone *does* find out—" he looked long and hard at the other man "—I'll know who to blame. Do I make myself clear?"

"Perfectly."

"Good. I won't risk her happiness. I won't risk losing her the same way I lost my Elena. It's as though I'm being given a second chance, and this time I'm not making any mistakes."

"And when her husband orders her not to see you again?"

"That is something I'll worry about when it occurs."

The other man had a bad feeling about this. A very bad feeling.

That night Cassie was all alone except for the servants. She had an early and very lonely dinner, then wandered into Franco's library and curled up on the couch with a book. Of all the rooms in the villa, this was her favorite. There was something comfortable and lived in about it. The faint, clean smell of leather hung in the air. It was very much a man's room. More than that, it was very much Franco's room.

She tried reading, but her thoughts kept drifting to her husband. Where could he be? Was he all right?

She had been quietly worried about him from the day he had left. Now that worry was growing until it nagged at her constantly. Enzo was no help. Every time she asked him where Franco was, he looked at her as though she were an enormous inconvenience and informed her that if her husband had wanted her to know where he was, he would have told her. Thank you, Enzo.

Cassie forced her attention back to the book, determined to concentrate. And she did, for a long time. But as the minutes passed, her eyelids grew heavier and heavier until she finally gave up altogether, thinking that she'd just close them for a minute and then finish the chapter.

An hour later Franco walked into the library and put his briefcase on his desk. Several days' growth of beard shadowed his cheeks. After one week in an uncomfortable safe house taking testimony from Salvatore he was tired, but pleased. The information he'd gotten wasn't only going to imprison the man he was taking to trial; several others were going to be very surprised when the police came knocking at their doors. Now if they could just keep Salvatore alive for another two months, the case would be made.

Franco walked to the doors leading into the courtyard and, leaning his shoulder against the frame, stared out at the night sky. A cool breeze blew against his warm face. If he had been smart, he would have stayed the night in Rome. It was what he would ordinarily have done.

But these weren't ordinary times. There was an irresistible force drawing him back to the villa, and her name was Cassie. How often had he found himself thinking of her over the past week? More often than he was comfortable with. He had told her she wouldn't make a difference in his life, but he had been wrong.

A movement on the couch caught the corner of his eye and he turned his head to find the object of his thoughts lying there, sound asleep, a book open on her stomach. A smile touched his lips as he moved beside her and stood staring down, hungry for the sight of her.

After awhile, he leaned over and gently touched her cheek. "Cassie," he whispered.

Cassie moved her head and sighed. "Um?"

He trailed the back of his hand down her smooth cheek again. "Cassie, wake up."

She moved again and the book slipped unnoticed to the floor. Slowly she opened her eyes and found herself looking at her husband. A sudden light filled her face as she gazed up at him, and Franco's heart caught at the beauty of it. "You're all right," she said softly.

"Of course." He pushed her hair away from her face. "Why aren't you in bed? It's late." He glanced at his watch. "Or early, whichever you prefer." He leaned over and slid his arms under her.

"What are you doing?" she asked in surprise.

"I'm carrying you to your room." He started walking with her, and Cassie wrapped her arms around his neck, resting her cheek against his shoulder with a sleepy sigh.

"I missed you."

He didn't say anything for a moment as he carried her up the steps. Then, so quietly that she almost didn't hear it, he said, "I missed you, too."

He pushed open her door with his foot and walked across the room to lay her gently on the bed. Cassie kept her arms around his neck and gazed into his hazel eyes with sleepy, dark blue ones.

Franco pushed the dark hair from her forehead, then gently removed her arms from around his neck and placed a gentle kiss on the inside of each of her wrists before lowering them to the bed. "You shouldn't look at men like that, Cassie. It might give them the wrong impression."

"Even my husband?"

His eyes rested on her lovely mouth. "Especially your husband. I'm tired, and my resistance is low."

"So is mine," she said softly.

His mouth moved irresistibly closer to hers. Cassie raised her arms until her fingers tangled in his thick hair and pulled him gently closer. When his mouth finally touched hers she moaned softly at the delicious wave of warmth that washed through her body. Oh, she could get used to this.

Franco tenderly kissed her soft lips, and then raised his head and looked down at her. "I find myself in the awkward position of wanting to make love to my wife."

Cassie trailed the back of her hand down his beard-shadowed cheek. "Your wife finds herself in the awkward position of wanting to reciprocate."

He gazed into her eyes. "I don't want to sleep with you just because you're here and convenient."

"Is that all it would be?"

He paused, smoothing back her hair. "No." Then he rested his mouth against her forehead. "No," he repeated softly as he straightened and looked down at her. "Good night, Cassie." And he went to his room.

Cassie watched the door close and then touched her mouth with her fingertips, turning her head to stare at the ceiling. Marriage to Franco Luciano wasn't the way she had imagined it would be. She had expected it to be impersonal. She had expected him to be cool toward her. But what she was finding was that her husband was a warm, vibrant, intelligent man, and it would be easy to fall in love with him.

And he was attracted to her. Cassie closed her eyes and lay very still, her heart beating rhythmically. Was it possible that she was falling in love with him?

She smiled. If she was, it felt wonderful. And how could something that felt this good not be right?

Her smile faded and her eyes opened. Because it wasn't what he wanted. And she could never bring herself to force her feelings on him.

She rolled onto her side with a sigh and hugged her pillow to her breast. A sorry substitute at best.

Franco walked onto the balcony of his room and stood staring out at the night as he quietly smoked a cigarette. He had always been in such control of his own life. From childhood he had known what he wanted to do, and he was doing it.

But now there was Cassie, and he certainly hadn't counted on meeting—much less marrying—anyone like her. She was different from any woman he'd ever met. Everything about her enchanted him, even her sometimes annoying curiosity. He was drawn to her; how could he not be? Not only physically, but emotionally. She touched something in him that no woman had ever touched before. He wanted to know her better, and yet he was afraid to do so. It was already obvious to him that letting her go when the time came was going to be difficult enough without complicating matters. And he would have to let her go. She might be half-Italian by blood, but she was all-American by nature. Creative, outgoing, and very much her own person. She could never be completely happy in Italy.

And she couldn't be completely safe being married to him. He would never allow what had happened to his mother to happen to Cassie. Never.

He flicked his cigarette over the balcony and leaned his elbows on the railing as he tiredly ran his fingers through his thick hair. A self-mocking smile curved his mouth. How ironic: For the first time in his life he'd found a woman he knew in his heart he was capable of loving and he couldn't have her, because having her meant putting her life in jeopardy.

Chapter Six

The next morning Cassie knocked on the closed library door.

"Come."

She opened it and found Franco sitting behind his desk, writing on a legal pad. He looked up, his eyes warm. "Good morning," he said, leaning back in his chair and tossing his pen onto the desk.

A delicious shiver wound through Cassie as she sat casually on the edge of his desk.

"What brings you downstairs so early?"

She picked up the pen and tapped it on the pad. "I have some things I'd like to discuss with you."

Franco put his hands behind his head. "This sounds serious."

"Oh, no, not really. First of all—" she took a deep breath "—I'd like to apologize for last night. My only excuse is that I was tired and not completely myself."

He lifted an expressive brow. "That's your only excuse?"

Cassie's quick smile flashed shyly. "It's the only one I'm using for now."

"Ah. And secondly?"

"Secondly, I was wondering if there's a spare room in the villa I could use as a studio. I know I'm not going to be here long, but I can still do some work."

Franco grew thoughtful. "I can think of one that would be perfect. It has lots of windows and catches both the morning and evening light."

"Which one is that?" She couldn't remember seeing anything like that on her tour of the villa.

"It's what you would call the attic. I'll show it to you later." He studied her serious face. "What else?"

She smiled. "How do you know there's something else?"

"I find I know a lot about what you're thinking just by looking at you."

"I'll have to work on that."

"Don't. It's one of the things I like most about you."

Cassie's cheeks grew pink, though her eyes met his unflinchingly. The man was charmed. "Actually, there is something else. I'd like you to give me a little more freedom."

He lifted a questioning brow.

"I don't like having to take Enzo with me wherever I go. It's not always convenient for him to follow me around, and I honestly don't think it's necessary."

"But I do."

"And I think you worry too much. If anyone has a security problem, it's you, not me. There's no reason for Enzo to have to go horseback riding with me. Or to follow me in his car whenever I drive off the property. I feel suffocated.''

Franco rose and walked to the open doors. The fountain was working this morning and the relaxing sound of the water whispered through the library. He sympathized with her. No one knew better than he how inconvenient it was having another person with you all the time. "Perhaps you're right," he surprised her by saying. "I'll allow you to go riding and driving without Enzo, but with the stipulation that whenever you come to the city, Enzo or someone else comes with you." He looked at her sternly. "Understood?"

"Understood. And thank you." She hesitated for a moment. "Speaking of riding, I'm going out a little later this morning. Would you like to come with me?"

"I would, if you can make it this afternoon rather than this morning."

"Done. Just come get me when you're ready." When Cassie left the library, she stood in the foyer and closed her eyes. How long was she going to be able to live near him without blurting out how attractive she found him? For the first time in her life she wanted to flat-out, no-holds-barred make love to a man. And if he could read her the way he said he could, she was going to have to watch herself very closely.

"Hello, sister."

Cassie jumped and found herself looking into Taddeo's amused eyes. "Where did you come from?"

"Not, unfortunately, the place where you just were in your thoughts. I think I might have enjoyed myself enormously.''

Cassie clicked her tongue. "Don't you ever think about anything else?"

"Not if I can help it. Anything interesting going on around here?"

Cassie frowned and wrinkled her nose. "Not particularly."

Taddeo smoothed her forehead with a gentle finger. "Frowning causes wrinkles."

Cassie smiled. "Listen, Taddeo, Franco just told me about an attic room with lots of windows that he feels would make a good studio. Do you know how to get to it?"

"You bet I do. We used to play there as children." He led the way up the stairs and down a long hall to what Cassie had assumed was a closet, but what turned out to be another staircase, leading to an enormous room. It was bright with the morning light, just as Franco had said it would be. But it was a mess. It would take a week just to clean it up. The dust on the wooden floorboards and everything else in the room was several decades thick. Old trunks had been left there without any particular order in mind. Furniture, discarded because of the changing tastes of the Lucianos over the years, was everywhere. And, of course, there were the ever-present cobwebs.

Taddeo looked around distastefully. "For reasons that escape me now, I loved this place when I was a child."

"Stop being so cynical. Of course you did." Cassie went over to a window and ran her finger through the dust. "Any child would like it up here. There's lots of food for the imagination."

"You'll need an army to clean it up."

Cassie shook her head as she gazed around the room with her dark blue eyes. "I don't think so. It's not really dirty, just dusty. Maria and I could probably have it ready in a few days."

Suddenly Taddeo struck an absurd pose and looked at Cassie out of the corner of his eye. "What do you think? Portrait material?"

Cassie laughed. "More caricature than portrait."

He dropped the pose. "I'm serious. Would you do a portrait of me?"

"Only if you pay me."

He shook his head. "Cassie, Cassie, Cassie. You would make your own beloved brother-in-law pay for a portrait? What's the world coming to?"

Cassie grinned at him, not at all defensive. "You can moan all you like, but I can't afford to paint anybody's portrait simply for the fun of it until I've repaid my debt to Franco."

"All right," he agreed. "How much? With a discount, of course."

"Five thousand dollars—with a discount, of course."

Taddeo's eyes widened. "You value your skill highly."

"If I don't, who will?"

"Good point."

"I thought so."

"Unfortunately, I think I'll have to settle for a snapshot." He winked at her and took one last look around the attic. "Let's get out of here before I start sneezing."

Taddeo looked at his watch when they were back downstairs. "What are you going to do with the rest of your day?"

"Franco and I are going riding this afternoon. Other than that, not too much."

"Would you like to have dinner with me?"

She hesitated. If Franco was going to be there, she'd prefer to eat with him. "Well, I don't really know...."

"I have it on good authority that my brother has a business dinner scheduled in Rome."

Cassie tried not to look disappointed, but her effort was a miserable failure. "Oh. Then yes, I guess dinner with you would be nice."

"Your enthusiasm is underwhelming," he said dryly.

Cassie smiled apologetically. "I didn't mean it that way."

"Of course you did, and that's all right. I need a little rejection now and then. It keeps me on my toes." Taddeo looked at her for a long moment. "I really do wish I had been the one to marry you, for however brief a time. It would have been an honor."

Cassie's smile warmed her eyes. "Thank you. I like you, too."

Taddeo kissed the top of her head and walked away from her and out the door with a negligent wave of his hand.

"Cassie."

Her heart leaped at the sound of Franco's voice behind her. She turned with a smile. "Hi. Ready to go riding?"

"I'm afraid I can't." He sounded genuinely disappointed. "I just got a call from my office. There are some things I need to take care of."

"That's all right. Really."

He put his hand under her chin and raised her face to his. "I was really looking forward to spending the afternoon with you."

Cassie's eyes rested on his mouth. "Some other time, perhaps."

"Count on it."

Enzo came up to them then. Franco gazed into her face a moment longer, then dropped his hand and turned to the bodyguard. They spoke in Italian, but Cassie didn't even try to follow what they were saying. She just stood there, staring at her husband. He wore tan slacks and an oversize white cotton shirt, open at the neck and with the sleeves rolled halfway up his forearms. It was a casual style that suited his tall frame perfectly, apparently achieved without conscious planning, and that, frankly, made it even more appealing. She couldn't stand men who appeared as though they spent hours preening in front of a mirror.

When he and the bodyguard finished talking, Enzo handed him some papers and left. Franco flipped through them. "Did you look at the attic?" he asked without looking at her.

"I did. And I like it."

"Good. Is there anything you want done to it to make it into your studio?" he asked almost absently, still looking through the papers.

"Only cleaning, and I can do that myself with some help from Maria."

"Well, if you need anything, just ask." Then he walked away from her and back into the library.

Cassie smiled ruefully to herself and started up the stairs to her room. There was nothing quite so gratifying as being the center of attention.

An hour later she was at the stables, saddling a beautiful black mare. It was another perfect day, warm—but not too warm—and bright. The sky was a remarkable blue, with giant white puffs of cloud floating lazily overhead. An insect buzzed by her ear and she brushed it away as she mounted the mare and headed in no direction in particular at a comfortable trot. Every once in a while she would give the mare her head and they'd race across the brown grass of the fields like the wind itself.

She found an almost-dry riverbed a few miles from the stables and decided to stop there, unsaddling the mare and letting her rest in the shade to nibble on what grass she could find. Cassie sat under a tree, too, leaning against the trunk, her sketch pad on her lap. She drew the scenery for a time, but after a few attempts, she found herself sketching Franco's face over and over. She lost all track of time and her surroundings and it was with some surprise that she noticed the sky growing dark and the rumble of thunder in the distance. A quick look at her watch told her that it was only six o'clock, much too early for it to be this dark. A drop of rain fell on her upturned face. It felt nice, but she didn't want to get caught out here in the middle of a storm. With quick movements, she saddled the suddenly jumpy mare and hoisted herself into the saddle. The rain had begun to come down harder and the thunder was closer. The sky went from being simply darkened to being black, and it was hard to make out the way back to the stables. Cassie always relied on landmarks like trees or rocks, but she couldn't see them now. What she finally did was let the mare lead the way. She knew the way back better than Cassie ever would.

The rain grew heavier, soaking Cassie completely, stinging her shoulders right through her blouse and running down her face and into her eyes. Lightning flashed through the sky above them and a crack of thunder sounded like a shotgun in the night. The already nervous mare bolted, running headlong, completely out of control. Cassie held on as best she could, but the saddle was slippery from all the water, as were the reins. The frightened mare was completely unresponsive to anything Cassie did.

She felt herself slipping. There was no way she could stay with the mare, and she tried not to think about what she had to do even as she loosed her feet from the stirrups. It was always better to leave a horse voluntarily than to get caught and dragged. She quickly wrapped the reins around the saddle horn so that they wouldn't trip the horse, then, with a determined set of her jaw and a silent prayer, kicked down on the saddle and threw herself free of the fear-crazed mare, landing on the hard ground with a thud that left her with a pain in her shoulder and struggling to draw air into her lungs. It was well over a minute before she could breathe normally.

Cassie slowly got to her feet, rubbing her sore shoulder. Rain was coming down in sheets, but there was nowhere she could take shelter. Not knowing what else to do, she followed the direction in which the mare had run. Frequent flashes of lightning sliced the dark sky and lit her path, but some of it seemed a little too close for comfort. The cracks of thunder that immediately followed shook the earth beneath her feet. The air had cooled considerably and a rising wind blew the rain into her face, chilling her to the bone.

About half an hour after she'd parted company with the mare, another flash of lightning showed Cassie the same cottage she had followed Enzo to the week before, only fifty yards away. Still clutching her shoulder, Cassie ran to it, stopping only when she reached the door. It wasn't locked. She pushed it open and then slammed it shut against the driving rain, leaning her back against it and panting as a puddle formed around her feet.

After a moment she moved away from the door and looked for a light switch. She found one not far away and flipped it up. Nothing happened. She flipped it up and down and up and down, and still nothing happened. The power was out. Great.

The next flash of lightning showed her a fireplace with a fire laid and ready. Which would have been perfect, if she'd had a match. "I knew I should have taken up smoking," she told the empty room in disgust as a shiver rolled through her wet body. "What good are clean lungs if you die of pneumonia?"

She stumbled around the room, trying to remember where things were. She found the desk and rummaged blindly through the drawers, looking for a lighter or matches, anything. No luck. She slammed the last one shut, close to tears. She was cold, hungry, her shoulder hurt, and she allowed herself the momentary luxury of feeling sorry for herself. She supposed she should try to get back to the house. She knew how to get there from here, and people would be worried about her. But nothing on earth would move her to go back out into that storm.

She felt her way along a wall to the bedroom, in search of a blanket, and she swore softly under her breath when another flash of lightning showed her that the bed had been stripped down to the mattress. Again she blindly felt her way along the walls, searching for a closet where linens might be kept. Nothing. No closet; no trunk; no chest of drawers.

Swearing softly under her breath, she went back into the living room. Her shivering was getting worse rather than better. She had the delightful choice of stripping off her wet clothes and standing around stark naked in the cold air or leaving the wet clothes on in the hope that her body heat would eventually dry them out and keep her warm.

She opted for leaving them on, and curled herself into a ball on the couch with her arms tucked between her legs and her breasts. How long she lay like that she had no idea. The storm raged on, occasionally lighting the room. The sound of the hard rain on the roof was surprisingly relaxing, almost like white noise. Cassie drifted in and out of sleep, but she couldn't shake the chills that now racked her body.

Suddenly she became alert. There was a noise outside that had nothing to do with the storm. It could be someone coming to find her. It could also be someone coming to find the informant who had been here. She moved stealthily to the fireplace to get a poker, and then to the door, where she stood quietly with it raised over her head, her teeth gritted against the pain it caused her shoulder, to strike whoever it was if she didn't know him.

And she waited, her breath held. The rain and thunder seemed to have grown even louder, and their combined noise filled the cottage.

There was a flash of lightning, and a voice suddenly cut across the room. "So there you are."

Cassie screamed and the poker fell to the floor with a metallic clatter. She leaned against the wall and put her hand over her pounding heart. "For God's sake, Franco."

He moved toward her through the dark. "I wasn't sure who was in here, so I came through a window in the bedroom. Are you all right?"

"Of course I'm not all right," she managed to say through gritted teeth, shivering. "I nearly suffered a massive coronary just now."

He put his hands on her shaking shoulders. "My God, Cassie, you're freezing."

"I got caught in the rain," she explained, her voice quavering with the cold that had invaded her body. "How did you know to come looking for me?"

"When the mare came back to the stables without you, Taddeo called to tell me you were missing. I've been out looking for you for the past two hours."

"But how did you know to come here, particularly?"

"It's shelter, and you knew where it was. Only an idiot would stay out in weather like this."

"Thank you for that tender compliment," she said dryly. And her tone was the only dry thing about her.

"Don't get cocky, woman. I have a few other choice things to say to you." His hands tightened on her shoulders and Cassie gasped in pain.

He let go immediately. "What's wrong?"

"My shoulder. I hurt it when I jumped from the horse."

He ran his fingers over it in the dark, pausing only when she gasped again. "I think it's a bad bruise. Nothing appears to be broken."

He stripped off his rain slicker and then walked into the bedroom. "Get those wet clothes off, Cassie," he called out to her.

She tried, but her hands were shaking so badly she couldn't get the buttons through the holes. When Franco came back from the bedroom he dropped whatever it was he was carrying onto the floor and gently brushed her hands away. Wordlessly, he unbuttoned her blouse, and the warmth of his hands as they brushed casually against her breasts penetrated the wet cotton, sending a very different kind of shiver through her. When he had undone the last button, Franco slid his hands inside the blouse and slipped it from her shoulders. Cassie was surprisingly unembarrassed. Perhaps it was because the dark covered her as well as any fabric—or perhaps it was because she was so at ease with this man that there was nothing unnatural about it.

Franco bent to pick up a towel he had brought from the bedroom and wrapped it gently around her shoulders. Moving behind her, he began vigorously rubbing her back and up and down her arms, always careful of her shoulder, to help get her circulation going.

It was wonderful. Cassie closed her eyes and enjoyed it. "Where did you find the towel?" she finally managed to ask, her voice vibrating to his massage. "I couldn't find anything dry. Not even a blanket."

"You didn't know where to look." He stopped rubbing her and took off his own dry shirt, then helped Cassie slip her arms into it. "Now take off your wet jeans and dry your legs."

He went into the small kitchen, his way lit by a flash of lightning, while she unfastened her jeans with trembling hands. They joined her blouse on the floor with a wet slap. Franco's shirt was a long one that came to the middle of her thighs. It smelled wonderful; not of cologne, but clean, like the man who had been wearing it.

He returned a moment later and handed her a snifter of brandy. "Drink that while I start a fire."

Cassie held the snifter cupped in her two hands, and it was with two hands that she raised it to her mouth and downed every drop. Sudden tears stung her eyes as the liquid burned its way down her throat.

A match flared in the darkness and soon flames were curling around the dry logs and the faint scent of pine filled the cabin. At first Franco's shadow was barely visible as he hunkered down in front of the fireplace, but as the fire began sending its dim, dancing light throughout the cottage, she could see him clearly as he moved the logs with a poker until the flames were high, sending real warmth into the room. The crackle of the burning wood mingled with the storm outside, somehow making the rolling thunder less threatening.

But the storm was secondary in her consciousness now. It was Franco who held her attention as he knelt in front of the fire, shirtless. He looked exactly as she had imagined, with the lean, sculpted body of an athlete. His shoulders were broad and they flowed into his powerful arms. When he stood up and turned around Cassie's heart flew into her throat. Her eyes wandered over his body; over the smoothly sculpted chest and muscled diaphragm that disappeared into his trousers.

A wave of dizziness washed over her. She hadn't eaten all day and the shivering had taken its toll on her energy. Franco swam before her eyes. She willed herself not to faint. She'd never fainted in her life, but her legs felt wobbly and suddenly wouldn't support her any longer. With hardly any warning, her knees buckled and she fell onto them.

"Cassie!" Franco was across the room instantly, on his knees before her. He put one hand on her to hold her steady while relieving her of the snifter with the other. His eyes bored into hers. "Are you all right?"

"I'm so cold...."

"Of course you are. Let me put you on the couch and then I'll get a blanket from the bedroom."

He started to rise, but Cassie caught his arm. "Just hold me, please."

Franco looked at her for a long moment, as though he knew exactly what this could lead to, and then slowly wrapped his arms around her trembling body and pulled her close to him. "You'll be warm in a minute," he said softly above her ear.

Cassie relaxed against him with a sigh that started at her toes, unaware of the tightening of Franco's jaw at her nearness. She was aware only of the warmth and security she felt when he held her like this. How long they remained thus, Cassie had no idea, but her shivering slowly subsided for the first time in hours, and then finally stopped altogether.

Franco put his hands gently on her shoulders and held her away from him as he looked into her eyes. "Better?"

She nodded. "Much, thank you."

A corner of his mouth lifted as he looked at her, kneeling there in his shirt with the buttons undone, her still wet hair straggling down her back. "You're welcome." He reached between them to fasten the shirt, but his hands brushed against her breasts in the process, and Cassie inhaled sharply. His hands stopped where they were as his eyes met Cassie's once again. She raised a hand and traced his carved mouth with a long finger, amazed at what a casual touch from this man could do to her.

Franco caught her hand in his and held it against his mouth, his eyes still on hers. He kissed her fingertip and then his mouth slowly made its way along the side of her finger and across her palm to the inside of her wrist. Cassie's lips parted softly on a whispered sound and her heart pounded as his mouth moved up the smooth skin of her arm to the sensitive place inside her elbow. His hands moved between them, unbuttoning the shirt he had just fastened, sliding a hand under it and slipping it from one of her shoulders. Cassie closed her eyes against the gentle warmth that filled her as Franco's lips caressed her now bare shoulder and moved ever so slowly up the side of her neck to linger behind her ear. And when his mouth finally captured hers, firmly and completely, Cassie was totally under his spell. She wrapped her arms around his neck as he lowered her to the floor and lay beside her, his body half covering hers. His tongue gently probed the sweet recesses of her mouth, drawing her further and further into him while his hand moved inside the shirt she was wearing, down over her flat stomach, around to the curve of her hip and down her thigh. Cassie was amazed at how sensitive her skin was to his lightest touch, and when his hand moved around to the inside of her thigh to lightly stroke her she gasped and pulled her mouth away from his.

Franco's hand stopped its stroking, but he kept it where it was as he looked down at her. His eyes were filled with a tenderness that took her breath away. Slowly, his mouth returned to hers, only to leave it again to caress the clean line of her jaw and throat, and to move ever so gently over the shoulder she had injured. The back of his hand brushed her raised nipple, sending a shiver through her that had nothing to do with the cold, but this time he didn't stop. His mouth caressed the soft swell of her breast as his hand moved down her side to her hip, pulling her more tightly against him until she could feel his desire pressing strongly against her. Then his mouth found the sensitive peak of her breast and gently flicked it with his tongue before covering it completely and sucking.

Cassie moaned softly. Her fingers tangled in his thick hair, pulling him more tightly to her as she arched against him. He raised himself above her for a moment and looked into her eyes before lowering his body onto hers and pressing against her breasts with his bare chest. His mouth came down on hers again, but this time there was a difference. He rolled onto his side, pulling Cassie with him so that they were facing one another. With infinite gentleness, he pushed her dark hair behind her ear and gazed into her lovely face. "Do you have any idea how much I want to make love to you?"

Her cheeks flushed with delicate color. "Do you have any idea how much I want you to make love to me?"

He trailed the back of his hand down her smooth cheek. "Hussy," he said softly.

Cassie just smiled.

But Franco grew serious, and her smile faded. "You understand, Cassie, that what's happening between us must stop here. We can't take this any further."

"But why, if it's what we both want?"

He kissed her forehead and then leaned his against hers, his thumb toying with the corner of her mouth. "Cassie, when I asked you to marry me I never bargained for this."

"For what?"

"That I would fall in love with my wife," he said softly.

She pulled slightly away from Franco, not sure she'd heard him correctly. "You're in love with me?"

"I've known a lot of women, Cassie, but I've never felt for any of them what I feel for you."

Her mouth parted softly. "Then why did you stop?"

"If you had been any other woman, we would have made love tonight. But with you it's too important a step. It has to be right for both of us, and tonight it isn't. You and I have a lot of thinking to do."

"I don't understand...."

"Oh, Cassie," he said softly as he rubbed his cheek against hers. "Nothing like this was supposed to happen between us." He raised his head and gazed down at her. "You were supposed to live here for a short time and then leave, and all without disturbing the world I've made for myself. But that's not the way it's working out."

Cassie's eyes searched his carved face as best they could in the firelight. "I think I've fallen in love with you, too."

Franco suddenly got up from the floor and walked to the fireplace to stare silently into the flames. "I don't know what to do, Cassie."

Cassie sat up and hugged her knees to her breast.

Franco dragged his fingers through his hair. "We're two completely different people." He turned to look at her. "We're not even the same nationality."

"I'm part Italian."

"Italy, for you, is a nice vacation, but to live here for a lifetime? I don't think you'd be happy. It's very different from what you're used to."

"I know that, but I'm capable of adjusting."

"And what about my work? Are you capable of adjusting to that?"

She didn't want to answer; she hated what he did. She hated wondering if he was going to make it through the day every time he left the house.

"So you see," he continued, "we have a lot to think about."

She took a deep breath and looked up at him. "So what do we do now?"

Franco came and hunkered down in front of her. "We get to know each other better. We find out if it's possible for us to build any kind of life together before we make love." He gazed into her eyes. "Because once we've made love, Cassie, I don't think I'll be able to let you go."

Her heart ached. She had a feeling she couldn't explain that things would never work out for them.

"So we pretend that tonight never happened?"

"For now."

She rose and walked over to the fireplace to stare into the flames. She stood in silence for a long time, then turned back to Franco. "Very well. Tonight never happened. Even though we both know that it did," she said softly.

Chapter Seven

Cassie dabbed at her canvas, but her heart wasn't in it. The man she was painting watched her curiously and finally broke his pose to move toward her, taking the brush from her fingers and the palette from her hands and laying them on the ground. Then he took her by the arm and led her to a chair under a tree and sat next to her, her hand in his. "Cassandra," Alessandro Forli said quietly, "what has been troubling you these past days?"

She tried her best to smile. "Nothing."

He didn't believe her for a moment. "There is trouble between you and your husband?"

Cassie looked at him in surprise.

"Is it because you are doing this work for me?"

"There's no trouble between us, and he doesn't know that I'm painting your portrait."

"I see. But if he found out he would be annoyed."

"Oh, I think that's putting his reaction mildly."

"So why did you agree to do it?"

She tilted her head as she looked at him. "The truth?"

"Naturally."

"Curiosity. Franco told me about you the day we had lunch near the Pantheon. I'd never met anyone like you before, so when you sent the wedding present it seemed a perfect opportunity."

He smiled at her. "If I had a glass of wine, I would toast your curiosity. Your presence in my home has been thoroughly enjoyed."

"Thank you. I appreciate the chance you've given me to get to know you a little."

He raised a silver brow. "A little?"

"A little. I don't know anything about you at this moment that you don't want me to know. You're a man with a lot of secrets."

His smile grew wider. "I like you, Cassandra Luciano."

"I like you, too. You're a better person than you think you are, you know."

"What makes you believe that?"

"Your eyes. Eyes never lie about what's inside a person."

"Ah."

"Do you have any family?" she asked.

His eyes narrowed. "Why?"

"Because you've never mentioned a wife or children in any of the sessions we've had. Most of the people I paint love to talk about their families."

"I'm sorry if I disappointed you. Yes, I once had a family. An English wife and one daughter. They're both dead now."

Cassie's heart went out to him. He suddenly looked very old. "I'm sorry."

He lifted his shoulders. "These things happen."

"What about grandchildren?"

His eyes touched hers. "I have two."

"They must give you great pleasure."

He said nothing, then changed the subject abruptly. "Would you like to continue with the portrait now or quit for the day?" he asked.

Cassie looked up at the clear sky. "I think we've done enough for today. The light is changing."

He rose and pulled her up with him. "Then I'll see you again tomorrow, same time." He looked down into her lovely face. "That is, if you'll be returning."

Cassie should have said no. She knew deep in her heart that she should never have taken this commission in the first place, but the more time she spent with Alessandro Forli, the more she liked him. It didn't seem to matter what he did for a living; the man she was painting was a good one. It showed in his face, in his eyes. She wanted to finish the portrait. "I'll be here."

He squeezed her hand. "Good." Then he turned away from her and went into his villa.

After packing up her supplies and handing them over to a servant to keep until the next day she went to her car and started out on the twenty-minute drive home. She didn't notice the car that slowly followed her, the same car that had been following her every day since she'd started coming to Alessandro Forli's home.

When she got home Maria met her at the door, all excited. "Your husband has been calling you. You must call him back right away."

Cassie put her shoulder bag on a chair in the foyer. She looked remarkably calm for someone whose heart had just leaped into her throat. Ever since they had been together at the cottage a few days before he seemed to be avoiding her by coming home late and leaving early in the morning, before she rose. "Did he tell you what he wanted?"

"No. Only that it was important that he talk with you. I put his number by the telephone in the library."

Cassie walked into the library and sat down behind the desk. She picked up the telephone receiver and stared at it for a long time before finally taking a deep breath and dialing. Franco answered the phone himself, and again her heart leaped. "Hello, Franco. This is Cassie. Maria told me you've been trying to reach me."

"I have."

"Why?"

There was a small pause. "I contacted the American judge this morning about your custody of Sam. He said that he expects to make a ruling sometime in the next week or ten days, and I got the impression that the ruling would be in your favor, rather than your aunt's."

Cassie closed her eyes tightly and then opened them again. "Thank heaven for that."

An unasked question hung in the air between them until Cassie dared to ask it. "What about our annulment?"

"The papers have been drawn up so that we can file them as soon as we receive official notification of his judgment—if that's what we choose to do."

Cassie's teeth tugged at her lower lip. "I see."

A silence fell across the telephone wire. Then, "We need to talk, Cassie. We need to spend some time together."

"I know. But it's a little difficult when you're never here."

"It's more difficult when I'm there. I can't look at you without wanting to make love to you."

That made her smile. "Are you coming home tonight?"

"I'd like to, but I can't. I have a late dinner meeting and afterward I think I'll just stay at my apartment."

"Oh." There was a world of disappointment in that one syllable.

"But tomorrow I'm taking the day off and I'd like to spend it with you."

Her heart lifted. "I'd like that, too."

There was another silence.

"Cassie?"

"I'm still here."

"I do love you. I wish things between us could be less complicated."

"I love you, too," she said softly.

"Good-bye."

"Good-bye." She listened to the click at the other end of the line and sat there for a long time before finally hanging up.

"Hi, Cassie."

She looked up to find Taddeo standing in the doorway. "What has you looking so sad and happy all at the same time?"

"Your brother." But she didn't elaborate, and he didn't probe. "What have you been up to? I haven't seen you around here for a couple of days."

He wiggled his eyebrows. "A gentleman should never kiss and tell."

Cassie shook her head. "You're as bad as a tomcat I once had."

"One can only try. What are you doing for dinner tonight?"

She glanced at the telephone. "Nothing."

"Want to go out with me?"

A genuine smile lit her lovely face. "You're on a real winning streak right now with women. I'd hate to be the one who breaks it."

"Don't worry about it. I'm due for a rest."

Cassie laughed out loud. "In that case, I'd love to. Where should we go?"

"Some place in the city." He grew thoughtful for a moment. "Do you like to dance?"

"I love it."

"Good. I know the perfect spot."

"What should I wear?"

"Something exquisite."

"I've got that. What time?"

He glanced at his watch. "Well, it's seven o'clock now. Can you be ready by eight?"

Cassie rose from behind the desk and walked over to Taddeo, reaching up on tiptoe to kiss his cheek. "I can and will."

Taddeo gave her a quick hug. "I hope my brother keeps you around here for a while."

Cassie hummed as she went upstairs. She knew exactly what she was going to wear and went right to it in her armoire. It was a cornflower-blue silk dress that left her shoulders bare and flared out from a narrow waist to just above her knees. The color was perfect for her. When she put it on she turned in a circle in front of her mirror and watched the dress fly out. It was made for dancing. Then she put on a little makeup and brushed her hair so that it hung smoothly past her shoulders.

When she was finished she stared at her reflection in the mirror and her smile slowly faded. If only it were Franco she was meeting for dinner. With a sigh, she turned away.

At exactly eight o'clock she went downstairs. Taddeo gave a long, low whistle and held out his arm. "Shall we?"

"Let's."

He tucked her neatly into his car and they were off. Taddeo glanced at her profile every once in a while as he drove. "What have you been doing with yourself lately?" he finally asked.

Cassie turned her head and smiled at him. "Nothing in particular. Why do you ask?"

"Because you're gone in the afternoons."

"Oh, that. I've been painting."

"Anything in particular?"

"Something very particular."

"Which you're not going to tell me about."

"That's right."

He shook his head. "There's nothing more frustrating than a mysterious woman," he told her as he parked in front of a modest-looking restaurant. The interior was also modest, but it was the people who made the place, not the decoration. All of them were superbly dressed. The women were all wearing their jewels. Groups of businessmen sat at several of the tables, talking intently. A man was playing the piano and some couples swayed to a slow rhythm on the small dance floor set in the middle of the restaurant. The maître d' seated them at a cozy table toward the rear and Taddeo handed him a generous tip.

"Do you come here often?" she asked, looking around.

"Whenever I can. This is my third time this week."

Cassie's eyes lit up. "No wonder he knew right where to seat you."

Suddenly she felt someone staring at the back of her head, and she turned to find herself looking directly into Franco's hazel eyes. Her heart stopped and then started again. The man next to him said something and Franco listened and responded, but his eyes never left her. She would have loved to have gone to his table to say hello, but he was here on business and she didn't want to interrupt. Cassie turned suspiciously to Taddeo. "Did you know your brother was going to be here?"

He looked at her with eyes far too innocent to be convincing. "How would I know that?"

"Something tells me you did."

He smiled at her as a waiter approached.

"There's nothing more annoying than a mysterious man," she said, repeating his words.

His smile just grew larger. "Would you like something to drink, Cassie?"

"Wine would be nice. Whatever kind you like."

He ordered, and the waiter returned a moment later with a bottle that he poured for them after Taddeo declined to taste it. He raised his glass to her. "To the loveliest woman in the room."

"How often have you used that line this week?"

He grew thoughtful. "How many times did I say I'd eaten here?"

"Three."

He nodded. "All right. Then this is the third time I've used that line this week."

Cassie nearly choked on the wine as her laughter bubbled. "Honestly, Taddeo, I don't know why I like you so much."

"I don't either. It's really rather disappointing. I used to think you had some taste."

"So did I."

Suddenly a hand lifted the hair from her shoulders, and lips lightly touched the back of her neck. Cassie's eyes widened and then closed for a moment as a delicious tingle went through her.

"Good evening, Mrs. Luciano," Franco's deep voice whispered next to her ear.

She turned her head and smiled up at him as he straightened. "Good evening."

"You didn't tell me on the telephone that you were coming here tonight."

"I didn't know."

"Would you like to join us?" Taddeo asked.

"I'd like to join my wife. You, I see enough of, little brother."

"Subtle, Franco. Subtle." He glanced casually at his watch and slapped his forehead. "You're never going to believe this, but I completely forgot that I was supposed to meet someone an hour ago." He tossed back his wine and got to his feet. "I know you must be terribly disappointed at having to spend the evening with only the two of you to entertain one another, but it can't be helped."

Franco took his seat. "We'll try to muddle through."

Taddeo winked at Cassie and was gone.

Cassie smiled at the man sitting across from her. "I think we've been set up."

"Remind me to thank him."

"What about the men you're with?"

"We've finished our business."

"So, it's just the two of us."

"Give or take forty people." His eyes drank in her face. "Dance with me, Cassie."

Her answer was in her eyes. He rose and took her hand, then led her to the dance floor.

It was rather crowded, so they couldn't do much moving, but from the moment Franco pulled her into his arms, she wouldn't have cared if they were standing still.

He held her even closer, until their bodies melded together as they swayed to the soft music. Franco's hand was warm on her back. Between that and the way his body moved against hers, Cassie didn't stand a chance. She tilted her head back and met his gaze with all the desire she felt reflected in her eyes.

Franco stopped dancing and stood looking down at her.

"Let me stay with you tonight," she said softly. "It's right. We belong together."

Franco gazed at her a moment longer, then gently took her arm to help her through the crowd and walked her out the door to his car. Wordlessly, he shoved it into gear and drove through the night to his apartment.

When they were finally inside he closed the door and turned to her in the darkness. "Cassie," he said, pulling her into his arms, "I want you to marry me again. And this time I want us to mean our vows."

Her mouth found his. "I'm beginning to think I meant them the first time," she whispered against it. His lips closed over hers as he picked her up in his arms and carried her to the bedroom to lay her gently on the bed. Piece by piece, their clothes fell to the floor.

He looked down at her, her dark hair spilling across the white pillow, her face framed by the moonlight coming through the windows. "You're mine, Cassie, just as I'm yours, and I don't want to lose you when you get custody of Sam."

"I'll stay for as long as you want me."

"Then you'll be here for a lifetime and beyond."

Her heart filled with a happiness she'd never known before as he lowered his head to kiss the soft spot between her breasts before capturing her mouth with his. He ran his tongue across her smooth teeth. "You taste good," he murmured. "Sweet."

Cassie rolled her husband onto his back and smiled softly down at him.

"What are you doing?"

"I don't know, precisely," she said provocatively, "but if it doesn't feel good, let me know and I'll stop." And she moved on top of him, pressing her body against his as her mouth moved down his throat and over his chest to the muscled wall of his stomach, lingering there briefly before moving still lower.

"Cassie," he moaned before catching her by the shoulders and pulling her up until she was at eye level with him. "Don't do that."

Cassie's teeth gently bit her lower lip as she smiled shyly at him. "Don't you like it?"

"Oh, I like it. I just don't need it."

Her smile grew as she discovered for the first time the power of her womanhood. Franco moved her onto her back and lay half on top of her. His hands gently held either side of her head as he looked deeply into her eyes before finally capturing her mouth with his. Cassie melted against him as her fingers dug into his strong shoulders, holding him closer. Everywhere he touched, her skin tingled, until her whole body ached with desire for him. A tension slowly built within Cassie, crying for release and only then did he make her truly his, with such gentle care and patience that she loved him all the more.

Franco raised himself over her and pushed her perspiration-damp hair away from her face. His eyes held something close to wonder as he gazed down at her. A slow smile touched his mouth as he rubbed his cheek against hers. "I love you," he whispered softly in her ear. He looked down at her again. "More than I ever thought I could love anyone."

Cassie felt such happiness that it frightened her. It couldn't last. Nothing this wonderful could last. He kissed her gently. "For once I can't tell what you're thinking."

She rubbed his cheek with the back of her hand. "That I love you so much it hurts. I'd heard that love could do that to a person, but I never believed it until now."

He caught her hand in his and held it to his mouth as he rolled onto his back, putting one arm around Cassie so that she could rest her cheek on his shoulder. Her fingertips moved gently over his chest. Silence fell between them for a long time. A contented, fulfilled silence.

"How many children do you want?" she suddenly asked him.

Franco smiled as he rubbed his mouth against the silky top of her head. "Ten. None."

"That's no kind of answer."

"It's the only one I have. I'm torn. On the one hand, I can't imagine anything nicer than a house full of little Cassandras. On the other hand—" he kissed her hair "—I don't want to share you with anyone, not even our children."

Cassie smiled and kissed his chest. "I was wrong. That's the best kind of answer."

Franco's arm tightened around her. "We'd better get some sleep. It's going to be morning soon."

Cassie rested her arm across his stomach, delighting in being so close to him. "Good night." A short time later her quiet, even breathing told him she was asleep.

Franco lay staring at the ceiling. His mind wouldn't shut down. Just before dawn he rose from the bed to stand near one of the windows that covered an entire wall, while he smoked a cigarette. He leaned his back against the frame and watched the woman he loved more than life itself while she slept. God, she was beautiful, inside and out.

He flipped the cigarette through the open window, looking at the building across the street as he did so. Suddenly something flashed and he dropped to the ground just as gunfire erupted, shattering the glass, bullets turning the plaster wall opposite the windows into dust. He pulled himself along the floor like a combat soldier until he reached the bed, then grabbed Cassie's arm and pulled her to the floor, covering her body with his own. The gunfire seemed to last for hours though in reality it was over in only about ten seconds.

And then there was silence. Neither of them moved as the smoke drifted around them. Sirens wailed in the distance.

Franco rolled off Cassie and pushed the hair away from her terrified face. "Were you hit?"

She shook her head.

"Are you sure?"

She nodded, beyond words.

He pulled her into his arms and held her tightly, then helped her sit up before rising himself and going to the phone. Fear had made Cassie breathless, and she panted as though she had just run a mile as she wrapped a sheet around herself and sat on the edge of the bed, her hand over her pounding heart.

He came back a moment later. "Enzo is coming to take you back to the villa."

She nodded and then looked up at him. "Why would anybody do something like that?"

Franco reached out a gentle hand to cup her cheek. "Because of who I am and what I do."

She swallowed hard. "I never realized...I never thought..." Cassie shook her head, unable to finish the sentence.

The sirens had grown louder until they stopped in front of the building. "Get dressed, Cassie. Enzo will be here shortly." And he walked out.

Methodically, Cassie picked her clothes up from the floor and dressed. A few moments later she walked out of the bedroom and saw her husband talking with uniformed police officers. He didn't introduce her, but came to her as soon as he saw her and, with his arm around her waist, walked her to where Enzo waited.

"Good-bye, Cassie."

She looked up at him. "Good-bye? Won't I see you later?"

He shook his head. "I think it's best if I stay as far away from you as possible for now. Away from everyone. At least until this case is finished."

"But..."

He silenced her with a kiss he had intended to be short and sweet, but he ended up pulling her into his arms and holding her tightly against him. "I don't know what I would have done if anything had happened to you."

Cassie pulled away and looked into his eyes. "Don't push me out of your life because of this."

He said nothing.

"Please, Franco. Don't let them do this to us. We belong together. Can't you see that?"

"What I see," he said softly, "is that you could have been killed tonight." He nodded toward Enzo, who took her arm and led her out to the waiting car. Franco's eyes followed her all the way, until the car was out of sight. Then he went back into his apartment. The police were moving quickly, taking notes on what they saw, asking him questions to which he had no answers—at least not answers he was going to give them. Very calmly, he put on a shirt and rolled the sleeves up, then went into the kitchen for a glass of water. He stood at the sink, deep in thought, the glass in his hand, and the rage he had felt since the shooting bubbled to the surface. His hand shook with it, tightening around the glass until it literally exploded. He stared at the blood from his cut hand, but there was no pain. He was too angry to feel pain. He jammed his hand under the running water to clean it, then wrapped a towel around it and, without a word to the police, left his apartment for a confrontation with the man he believed was responsible for what had happened.

Chapter Eight

Franco braked his car to a screeching halt in front of the gates of the villa. A man came out of a small guardhouse near the gates and looked at him with a frown. "What's your business?"

"I want to see Alessandro Forli."

"At six in the morning? You have to be crazy. He's sleeping."

"You call him now and tell him that Franco Luciano is here."

The guard's eyes narrowed. He knew the name. "Just a minute."

He went back to the guardhouse, but returned a moment later and opened the gates. "He says he'll see you."

Franco said nothing, but slammed his Ferrari into gear and sped down the narrow drive to the villa. As he walked up the steps, the floor-to-ceiling front door was opened by a servant who led him into an office. "Signor Forli will be right down. Please have a seat."

Franco was too angry to sit down. He paced back and forth like a caged tiger until the man he was waiting for appeared in the doorway, dressed in a silk robe over his pajamas.

The old man eyed his guest with less surprise than might have been expected. "To what do I owe the honor of this visit, Signor Prosecutor."

"You know damn well why I'm here. How dare you send your assassins to murder me in my home? In my bedroom, where my wife was sleeping? If you want me dead, then you come after me and leave my family alone."

The old man paled. "Cassandra—was she hurt? Is she all right?"

"No thanks to you." The gangster's familiar use of his wife's first name didn't register immediately.

Signor Forli sank tiredly into a chair. "Thank heaven for that." He looked up at his accuser, and there was no mistaking his sincerity. "Franco, as God is my witness, I know nothing of what happened."

"It could only be you, because you know as well as I do that I'm about to put one of your top men away for life."

The old man shook his head. "You know me, Franco. You know how I operate. This isn't my way. Genco is being tried by you because he was stupid. Stupid and greedy. As far as I am concerned, he is on his own. I would not interfere. It's not my way," he repeated.

Franco walked over to the window and dragged his fingers tiredly through is hair. His instinct told him the old man was telling the truth. But if that were so, who was behind the shooting? Genco himself? But he would never do that without the approval of Forli. Never.

Alessandro Forli walked up behind him and put his hand on the younger man's shoulder. "Franco, if I find out anything, I'll let you know."

Franco stared at the hand on his shoulder until the old man took it away. "Why would you lift a finger to help me? You and I are natural enemies, Alessandro. Your life would be much easier if I were out of the picture."

The old man shrugged. "If you weren't there to hound me, watching for any little mistake, then it would be someone else. With you, at least, I have some advantage."

"Which is?" Franco asked.

"That you and I are not so dissimilar as you think, my friend. We are both honorable men, in our ways. I have a certain respect for you, which I believe you also have for me. And I have a very good reason for wanting to keep you alive."

Franco waited.

"My granddaughter is in love with you."

A frown creased Franco's forehead. "Your granddaughter?"

"Cassandra."

Franco just stared at him. "Cassandra is your granddaughter?" he asked in disbelief.

"I have no reason to lie about such a thing."

"How do you know this?"

"Come with me." Alessandro started from the office, but turned back at the door to his still unmoving guest. "Please, come. I'll show you how I know."

Franco followed him down the hall to a large library. Over the fireplace was a portrait of a woman who could have been Cassandra. The clothes were of a different era, but there was no mistaking the stunning blue eyes and raven hair.

Alessandro moved close to the portrait and looked up at it. "Beautiful, wasn't she? This was my daughter, Elena. She got her blue eyes from her English mother." Then he turned to Franco. "So, you see how I know. And now you know, too." He sat on the edge of the bed with a tired sigh. "Cassandra has been coming here every day for the past week to paint my portrait. We've become friends. She's a granddaughter to be proud of."

Franco stood staring at the portrait. "Does she know?"

"That I'm her grandfather?" He shook his head. "And I would prefer that she not find out. I don't want her hurt the way her mother was. That's why I'm willing to help you find out who's behind the shooting this morning. Not because I particularly care about keeping you healthy, but because I don't want to see my granddaughter caught in the cross fire."

Franco studied him with a quiet intensity that made even Alessandro Forli flinch. "And what is it that you want in return for that help?"

"I could bargain with you, I suppose, but I won't this time. I'll do this for my granddaughter."

He walked Franco to the front door. "You and I might be, as you say, natural enemies, and enemies we will remain, but there is one thing in this world that binds us inextricably together: Cassandra."

Franco eyed him steadily, then left without another word. He sat behind the steering wheel for a long time and finally brought his fist down on it. It was like a nightmare. The woman he loved was the granddaughter of a man he'd been trying to imprison for years. He was torn between wanting to tell her because she had a right to know and wanting to protect her from that knowledge.

And there was always the possibility that if she found out, she'd leave him, believing it to be in his best interests. And the one thing he'd discovered in the last twelve hours was that he couldn't lose her. He loved her too much.

He put the car into gear and drove back to the city, more slowly this time.

The old man watched until the car was out of sight. Then he called to his assistant. "I want you to get me in to see Genco."

"But nobody can see him."

Alessandro narrowed his eyes. "I—" he poked at his own chest "—am not nobody. I am Alessandro Forli. And you will get me in to see him so that I can tell him myself that if one hair on Cassandra Luciano's head is harmed, he will answer to me and, immediately thereafter, to God."

Cassie paced around the library, stopping to stare at the telephone every once in a while, as though willing it to ring. It was now past eight o'clock at night, and she hadn't heard from Franco all day. She had no idea what was happening, whether or not the men who had shot at them had been caught or at least identified; nothing. It was an awful feeling.

"Cassie."

She jumped and put her hand over her heart at the sound of her name. Taddeo stood in the doorway.

"May I come in?"

She smiled, relieved to see him. "Of course you may. It's your home."

"I saw Franco today. He told me what happened this morning." He shook his head. "I'm really sorry, Cassie. If I'd had any idea, I never would have left you last night...." He sat in a chair near the desk, and Cassie perched on its arm.

"You know, Taddeo, it's the strangest thing, but I feel almost as though I dreamed it. Everything happened so quickly."

"You do seem remarkably calm."

"I am. Shockingly so."

"Well, your husband isn't. He's mad as hell. I pity the people who did it if he catches them."

"I don't. They deserve everything they get."

Maria came into the library, obviously excited. "Signor Luciano is here. Up in his room."

Without excusing herself to Taddeo, Cassie ran out of the library and up the stairs to Franco's room, then stood in the doorway staring at the back of his head as he bent over an open suitcase. "Franco?"

He turned, and the look of love that shone from his eyes was all she needed to move into his arms. He held her tightly against him with one hand at her waist and the other at the back of her head, pressing her cheek against his shoulder. "Cassie."

She kissed his shoulder and then his mouth, and stood looking into his hazel eyes. "Why are you packing?"

"I'm going to be staying at a hotel in Rome until my apartment is repaired."

"Why not here?"

"Because I don't want what almost happened to you this morning to happen to anyone here."

He cupped her face in his hands and gazed at every feature, as though memorizing them. Cassie had a sudden sinking feeling. Somehow she knew what was coming next, but she asked anyway. "What's wrong?"

"Nothing is wrong. I'm just sending you away for a time. At least until this trial is over."

"No," she said calmly. "I won't go. I belong here with you."

The warmth in his eyes took her breath away. "No, you don't. You belong in America, safe with Sam."

"But we don't even have a place to go anymore."

He pulled some papers out of his pocket and handed them to her. "Yes, you do. I bought your home back from the couple to whom you sold it."

Cassie looked at the papers and then back at her husband. "That's not possible. They loved the house and would never have sold it."

He took the papers from her, unfolded them and then held them up for her to read. Sure enough. "How did you get them to agree to this?" she asked curiously.

"Let's just say I made them an offer they couldn't refuse."

"Oh," Cassie groaned at his choice of words. Then her smile faded. "I can't accept this."

"Why not?"

"It's too much. I already owe you enough to keep me painting for several years. With this on top of it, I'll never be able to repay it all."

His expression was tender as he cupped her cheek in his hand. "Cassie, I don't want your money for this. It's my gift to you and to Sam. It's your home and you should have it."

Her eyes searched his. "Why are you going to such lengths to get rid of me?"

Franco gently kissed her mouth. "I'm not trying to get rid of you, Cassie. I've just found you. I only want to keep you safe."

"And who's going to keep you from harm?"

"I'm a big boy, and I can watch out for myself a lot better if I'm not constantly worrying about you."

"And if I go," she asked softly, "when may I come back?"

"When the Genco trial is over."

"And what about when the next trial starts, and the one after that and the one after that? Are you going to send me away for all of them?"

He turned his back to her and began putting things into the suitcase. "I've been thinking about spending more time on my private practice."

Cassie's eyes narrowed. This didn't sound at all like the man who had told her only days earlier how strongly he felt about what he was doing. "Why?"

He went to his dresser and took out some things, then walked back to the bed and again bent over his suitcase, not looking at her once. "It's time. I've been doing this for five years. It's someone else's turn to get shot at."

"Franco?" She waited until he looked up at her. "What's going on?"

"Don't you think what happened this morning answers that?"

She shook her head, trying desperately to read his carved face. "For some people, perhaps. Not for you. Something else happened between when I last saw you this morning and now."

Franco took a deep breath and looked at her long and hard before finally pulling her into his arms. "Cassie, stop questioning everything I say or do. Now, please," he said against her hair, "as a favor to me, take Sam and go back to Illinois until this is over. I'll come for you when I can."

She held him tightly to her. All of her instincts were telling her not to go. But she couldn't bring herself to argue with him any longer. Willing herself not to cry, she moved away from Franco and sat down on the edge of the bed. "All right. When do you want us to go?"

He smiled at her, and the warmth sent a wave of desire through her. "Thank you, Cassie. I've made travel arrangements for the day after tomorrow."

He went back to packing. Cassie sat quietly next to the suitcase, occasionally pulling out something and refolding it for him, then setting it neatly back.

"Cassie?"

"Um?"

"Why didn't you tell me you were working on a portrait of Alessandro Forli?" he asked casually. Almost too casually, Cassie thought.

"I knew you wouldn't approve."

"If you knew that, why did you do it at all?"

"At first I was curious, and I also thought that perhaps I might see or overhear something that could help you."

"And then?"

She lifted her shoulders. "And then I did it because I started to really like the man. He's not a monster, you know."

Franco didn't answer that, but pulled her back into his arms. "You have such a good heart that you try to see good qualities in everyone else. They aren't always there, Cassie. Don't give away your trust too easily." His mouth searched hers with devastating gentleness.

He sighed against her ear. Then he released her. "I have to go now. I'll call you tomorrow."

Cassie attempted a smile, but it was tremulous at best. "Good-bye."

Franco pulled her into his arms again. "Oh, Cassie, don't look at me like that. It won't be for long. And once I'm back in private practice, we won't have to go through this ever again."

Then he picked up his suitcase and walked through the door.

Cassie stood where she was for over a minute, staring at the empty doorway. Then she moved over to the window and looked out. Her hand rested lightly on the frame. Franco emerged from the villa a moment later, threw his suitcase into the car trunk and was about to climb behind the wheel, but he never got the door open. Somehow he sensed Cassie watching him. His eyes met hers for a long moment, and then he moved away from the car toward the villa and plucked a rose from one of the bushes against the house. He stood under the window and tossed it up, right into her hands. "I love you," he said softly.

Cassie's throat closed and tears stung the backs of her eyes. "I love you, too."

And then he left. She watched until the last particle of dust from his tires had settled, then sat on the edge of the bed sadly cradling the rose in her hand. She had the strangest feeling that something was about to go wrong between them. There was no logic behind the feeling. It was just a premonition. She had no doubts about Franco's feelings for her, and none about hers for him. But she wasn't happy and she didn't know why. She should be thrilled! He had all but promised her that he was resigning as special prosecutor. He would be safe. She wouldn't have to run from Italy.

But why this sudden decision of his? What was behind it? What was going on that she didn't know about?

She walked thoughtfully to her room and carefully pressed the rose between the pages of a book, which she then set on her dresser. Then, instead of going back downstairs where she would have to deal with people, she turned out the light and lay on Franco's bed.

The next morning she woke still tired, as though she hadn't slept. But after splashing some cold water on her face and changing her clothes, she felt a little better. She had some things she wanted to do today before leaving Italy, and one of them was seeing Alessandro Forli.

It was still early when she pulled up in front of his villa. A maid she knew let her in, but told her the signor was out and wouldn't be back for another hour. Cassie decided to wait.

She sat in the office for a while, but got bored and began wandering around a bit. The layout of his villa was surprisingly similar to Franco's. She peeked into the library and when she found no one there, went in to look at the books. Instead, she found herself looking at a portrait of her mother.

Cassie was shocked. There was no other word for it. She sat down in the nearest chair and stared at it in disbelief. Why would Alessandro Forli have a portrait of her mother hanging over his fireplace?

Unless she were the daughter he had told her about. Little things were beginning to fall into place. The way he had looked at her at the café. His reference to two grandchildren. His sadness when she'd told him of her mother's death. It all made sense.

Horrible, horrible sense.

And somehow Franco had found out yesterday. She had sensed that something had happened, and that's what it was. Why else would he suddenly be talking about a private law practice? It was because his wife presented him with an insurmountable conflict of interest. On every case involving anyone connected with her grandfather—she shook her head. Her grandfather. On every case involving anyone connected with her grandfather, Franco's integrity would be called into question.

Cassie gazed sadly at the portrait for a little longer, then decided to leave without seeing Alessandro Forli. She hadn't the faintest idea what to say to him now.

She got back into the Fiat, but instead of going

home, she found herself on the road to Rome and Katrina Luciano's apartment. The woman opened the
door herself and stared at Cassie for a moment before
speaking. "My dear, what a nice surprise!"

Cassie gave her a half smile and stepped into the
apartment. "Can we have a talk?"

"Certainly, certainly. Let's go out on the terrace.
It's too lovely a day to be cooped up inside."

Cassie followed her out and sat across the round
table from her. "I want you to tell me about my
mother."

As she had before, Signora Luciano seemed some-
what uneasy. "I've really told you all I could think
of."

"Except that her maiden name wasn't Asti. It was
Forli."

The older woman blinked at her in surprise. "How
did you find out?"

"I saw her portrait hanging in Alessandro Forli's
library this morning. Why didn't you tell me? I know
you knew."

"I did. You're quite right. I thought I was doing
what was best for you by not saying anything. If your
mother had wanted you to know, she would have told
you herself, rather than letting you believe you had no
family in Italy. She wanted no ties to her father. She
hated him and everything he stood for."

"Have you told anyone who I am?"

"No. Not even Franco. I think I would have if I'd
known he was going to marry you, but I never had the
chance."

"That explains the disapproval I sensed when he
brought me here for the first time."

"I'm afraid so. I do love you, Cassie. You're a delightful woman and it's obvious that my grandson is very deeply in love with you. But you compromise him simply by virtue of who your grandfather is."

"I know that."

"Have you decided what you're going to do?"

"Franco is sending Sam and me to America tomorrow. He assumes I'll be coming back here when he finishes the trial he's involved in now. I won't."

Katrina Luciano reached across the table and covered Cassie's folded hands with her own. "Are you sure that's what you want?"

"I'm sure that it's *not* what I want, but it's the only thing to do. He was talking last night about going back into private practice, but that's not where his heart is. He would only do it for my sake. And, of course, there's Sam. If this were to become public knowledge, my seven-year-old brother would become infamous throughout Italy. Life's hard enough nowadays without having to defend yourself against your grandfather's reputation."

"If you need anything, let me know."

"Thank you, but you've already done more than enough." She got to her feet. "I should be getting back to the villa before I'm missed."

Signora Luciano rose with her and kissed both her cheeks. "Take care of yourself."

"I will."

"And keep in touch."

Cassie smiled. "Good-bye."

When she got back out to the car Cassie sat there for a moment, trying to get her bearings. A lot had happened in the past few hours. She couldn't believe that she was actually going to leave Franco. Her heart cracked in half.

Chapter Nine

She drove off in her car, not noticing the car following her once again. About ten miles before she got to the villa the car came up behind her, passed her on the left and then whipped in front of her and slammed on his brakes. Cassie hit her brakes as well, but she never had a chance to stop. The front of her car crashed headlong into the rear of the other one. Her seat belt caught and held her tightly in place, but the impact left her shaken and angry. What kind of idiot was behind the wheel of the other car? She popped open her seat belt and reached for the door handle, but before she could open it, two men got out of the other car.

Cassie's heart stopped. She knew instantly that she was in trouble. One ran to the passenger side of the Fiat and opened the door to lean in while the other ran to the driver's side and tried to put a cloth over her nose. Cassie's instinct for survival replaced her civilized manners as she managed to bite the hand of the man with the cloth. He swore in a language she didn't recognize and grabbed her by the hair, but her adrenaline was so strong she didn't even feel it. All she knew was that she couldn't let them get her. The man on the passenger side was trying to grab her hands. She managed to get one of her legs free from under the steering wheel and smashed her sandaled foot into his face. She had the small satisfaction of seeing his look of shock and pain as his nose started to bleed.

And then the cloth was jammed against her face again and the fight left her. She tried to scream, but nothing came out. Cassie grew weaker and weaker from whatever they had put on the rag. Her eyes locked with the furious black ones of the man she had injured, and those eyes were the last thing she saw before unconsciousness overcame her.

Taddeo was driving along, humming to himself. It was a beautiful afternoon. Then he spotted an accident ahead and slowed down, finally stopping right behind the battered car there. It was still in the middle of the road. Taddeo put his flashers on, then climbed out of his car and walked up to the wreck. It looked like one of his brother's cars. He went around to the passenger side and opened the glove compartment to take out the registration. Franco's name was there. He gazed around the interior of the car. There was quite a bit of blood on the front seat, and a white cloth. He examined the cloth closely, wrinkling his nose at the strange odor.

Then he went back to his own car and used the mobile phone to call the villa. Maria answered.

"Maria, this is Taddeo. Do you know if anyone from the villa was using the red Fiat today?"

"No, I don't think so. That's the car the signora has been using lately, but she didn't go out this morning."

"Are you sure?"

"Of course."

"Would you check her room anyway?"

Maria set the receiver on the table and went upstairs. First she knocked on Cassie's door. Then, when there was no answer, she pushed it open. No one was there. She picked up the phone on Cassie's bedside table. "She's not here. And I just finished going through the house and I didn't see her. What's wrong?"

Taddeo's mouth formed a straight line. "I don't know. Call my brother, will you? Tell him to meet me on the road home. There's something here I think he should see."

"Yes, sir."

"And tell him to hurry."

Then he went back to the Fiat and stood with his arms folded across his chest and a sinking feeling in his stomach.

Franco arrived less than half an hour later and parked behind his brother. "What's going on?" he asked, striding over to Taddeo.

Taddeo handed him the registration. "I found your Fiat here, just the way it is now." He had trouble saying the next words. "I think Cassie was driving it."

Franco's face paled when he saw the blood on the seat.

"It looks as though someone pulled in front of her, causing the accident. The car didn't get in this condition all alone." He handed his brother the rag and Franco lifted it to his nose.

"Chloroform."

"I think she was snatched, Franco."

His jaw grew taut. "Where was Enzo?"

"You told her she didn't have to take him with her everywhere she went." Taddeo touched his brother's arm, feeling some of the pain he saw etched on Franco's usually stoic face. "I'm truly sorry."

Franco didn't respond, but looked into the car again. "It might not be Cassie," he finally said, grasping at straws.

Taddeo said nothing.

Franco handed him back the registration. "You wait here for the police while I go back to the villa. Perhaps there's been some word." He pushed the Ferrari to the limit going to the villa. He ran from his car, throwing the front door open and taking the steps two at a time to Cassie's room. He stood in front of her closed door for a long time, his breath coming fast. His eyes closed for a moment before he opened her door and stared into her empty room. But still he couldn't accept that she had been in that car. She must be somewhere in the house. He quickly turned to leave and nearly bumped into Maria.

"Signor, this just came for you." She held out a manila envelope.

Franco looked at it for a long, dread-filled moment before taking it from her and slowly opening it. He reached in and pulled out Cassie's simple wedding band, swallowing hard as he held it gently between his thumb and forefinger. He took a deep breath before pulling out the accompanying note and reading it. The maid watched, not understanding what was going on, but realizing it must be something horrible simply by the way Franco's shoulders had slumped and the sudden paleness of his face.

But then he changed, radiating such silent fury that Maria was frightened. "What does it say?" she asked, her eyes wide.

"They're terrorists. Cassie has been taken by terrorists. This has nothing to do with the Genco trial." He stared at the ring, then put it in his breast pocket and walked abruptly from the room and out to his car. He drove back to the wrecked Fiat. Police now swarmed over the area while Taddeo stood by and watched. Franco pulled up next to his brother and handed him the envelope through the car window. "Give this to the man in charge. I have to go see Alessandro Forli."

Taddeo took the envelope, but looked at Franco in surprise. "Alessandro Forli? Does he have something to do with this?"

"No, but he might be able to help me get her back."

Franco had no trouble getting through her grandfather's gate, and Alessandro Forli met him a short time later in his study. "This is getting to be a very bad habit of yours, Luciano. What will people say when they see you so much at my home?"

Franco didn't even hear what the man said as he turned to him. "I need your help."

The old man lifted an expressive brow as he sat down behind his desk. "*You* need *my* help. An interesting development, to say the least. And if it has to do with that attack on you yesterday, I've made inquiries, and so far I haven't found the men responsible."

"Cassie has been kidnapped."

There was a long silence as Forli digested what Franco had told him. "But that's not possible."

"It's more than possible. It's happened."

"But she was just here this morning."

"What time?"

"It must have been around nine o'clock. I wasn't here, and she waited for a time, but then left before I got back." He looked intently at the young man across from him. "Do you know who did this?"

"A terrorist group who wants some of its members released from prison in exchange for Cassie's return."

"The government will never agree to that."

"I know. That's why I'm here. You have contacts the police don't, and ways of getting information. If anyone has a chance at finding her before she's harmed, it's you."

The old man rose from behind his desk and paced back and forth, then stopped in front of Franco. "Why did they take Cassie? I don't understand."

"I'm the one who put each of the men they listed into prison."

"Do you have the note with you?"

"I gave it to the police."

"The police," Alessandro spat with disgust. "They will make a lot of noise and accomplish nothing. What exactly did the note say they'd do if the men aren't released?"

"They said they'd put Cassie on trial for *my* crimes against the people."

"And we both know how that farce will end."

"With her execution."

The two men looked at each other. Then the older one broke the silence. "I need some assurances from you."

Franco waited.

"If we will be working together, you will see some people in my home and hear things that could be held against me in a court of law. I want your assurance that when this is over and we have her back, you will forget everything you've heard and seen. We go back to square one."

Franco didn't have to think about it. "You have my word."

Alessandro Forli inclined his head, satisfied. The man standing before him was known throughout the underworld as a man of honor. He had never broken his word before. The old man began making phone calls as Franco went to stand by the window, watching and waiting. There was nothing else he could do.

Cassie felt sunlight touch her face. She slowly opened her eyes and blinked several times. Her head ached and her mouth was dry. When she tried to sit up she felt sick and fell back onto the cot. After a few more minutes she tried again. This time it was easier. She swung her legs over the edge of the cot and sat there looking around. She was in a place not much larger than an oversized closet. There were two windows with bars across them. The cot was the only furniture.

She stood up and walked to one of the windows. She was in the middle of a vineyard. No one else was around. What was she doing here?

Then the memory of yesterday came back. The accident. The cloth with the awful smell that had knocked her out. She had been kidnapped. But by whom? And why?

She heard the sound of an engine approaching on the small dirt road and she narrowed her eyes, staring into the distance, trying to see who it was. A Japanese van, churning up dust in its wake, pulled to a stop in front of the cabin. Her heart pounded as she straightened her shoulders and turned to face the door. Two men and a woman walked in a moment later, all of them carrying guns. No one said anything. One of the men—apparently the one she had kicked, because his nose was bandaged and she could see that he had two black eyes—pushed her none too gently back onto the cot and handed her a newspaper, opened to the front page, to hold just beneath her chin. Then he took her picture. The woman went out to the van and came back with a bag of food, which she tossed onto the floor.

Cassie had a hundred questions to ask, but she remained silent. Her eyes followed the man who had handed her the newspaper. He was young—no more than twenty-three or -four. And he wasn't Italian. He had more of a Middle-Eastern look about him. He looked at her scornfully, but Cassie's direct gaze was unflinching. She didn't want to seem frightened, though she quaked on the inside. His scorn turned to curiosity.

Less than fifteen minutes after they'd arrived, the trio left. Not a single word had been spoken by any of them. Cassie went to the window and watched them drive away, this time studying the license plate—for all the good it would do her.

She looked into the bag of food. There was a sandwich and a can of soda. She took the soda and left the food, then went back to the cot and picked up the newspaper. Its Italian headlines trumpeted the news of her kidnapping. She read every word, and for the first time understood what had happened to her. It was a relief not to be in ignorance any longer, but at the same time she almost wished she hadn't read it. She knew that the government would never release those people in exchange for her freedom. They had never given in to terrorists before. And she didn't know of anyone who had been put on trial by a terrorist group and found innocent.

Cassie leaned against the wall, holding the can of soda in both hands between her raised knees. She should have been hysterical. No one could have been more surprised by the absolute calm that filled her than Cassie. It was the same way she felt sometimes when she got on a plane and knew that her fate lay in someone else's hands. She had to trust that Franco would get her out of this. And she did. If it were humanly possible, he'd find some way to help her.

Then her thoughts turned to Sam. That poor little guy. First his parents and now this. What would he do without her? She wondered if the courts would leave him with Franco or force him to go to Aunt Emily....

Franco paced around his library. It was agony waiting for the phone to ring, wondering if Cassie were all right. For the first time since childhood, he wanted to cry.

Taddeo came in and closed the door behind him. He held an envelope in his hand. "This just came."

Franco ripped it open and pulled out a picture of Cassie holding that day's newspaper. He closed his eyes and breathed. At least she had been alive earlier today. He put the photo on his desk and he and Taddeo looked it over with microscopic attention. "She doesn't look injured," Franco said finally.

Taddeo had to agree. A smile curved his mouth. "If I know Cassie, she probably did something to one of them."

Franco couldn't smile. His eyes still studied the picture, looking for something; anything at all that might help them find her. But there was nothing, not a clue to be found anywhere.

Franco slammed his fist on the desk and swore. "So help me, Taddeo, if they harm one hair on her head, I'll murder them all."

"She'll be okay. Cassie's very resourceful."

"I know that. But these people..." He shook his head. "Why Cassie?"

"Her connection to you, obviously."

"But why not me? I would be a far better bargaining tool." He moved over to the window and stared out blankly.

"You love her very much, don't you?"

Franco was silent for a long time. Then his hollow eyes met his brother's. "Taddeo, if anything happens to her, I don't know what I'll do."

Taddeo put his hand on Franco's shoulder. "She'll be fine. I feel it in my bones."

The phone rang, and Franco grabbed it. "Hello."

"Franco, this is Alessandro Forli. I'm afraid that so far my people haven't come up with anything. How about the police?"

His heart sank. "Nothing."

"We'll keep at it until we find her. And we will find her."

"I know." He hung up.

"How long has it been since you've gotten some sleep?" Taddeo asked.

"The night before she was taken."

"That's been over forty-eight hours. You've got to rest or you won't be any good to Cassie or anyone else."

Franco was too tired to argue. He went to the couch and lay down, his forearm covering his eyes. But still he could see Cassie's lovely face.

Cassie heard the van coming the next day. She had done some thinking during the night, and if they followed a pattern of having her hold up a newspaper every day to prove that she was still alive, there might be a way to signal Franco. She didn't know where she was, but she had a license number. If she could just arrange her fingers on the newspaper in such a way that someone looking for clues would see that she was flashing numbers, it might help.

The van stopped in front of the small building. Cassie sat down on her cot and waited. A moment later the same three people came in. The man with the broken nose tossed a newspaper at her. Cassie had to bite her lower lip to keep from smiling. She opened the paper and raised it in front of her, carefully holding it so that the hand on the right side showed four fingers and the one on the left showed two. And this time, instead of looking into the camera, Cassie trained her gaze onto her right hand.

The fellow taking the photograph didn't notice anything out of the ordinary. Soon the terrorists left, and Cassie stood up and paced back and forth, a smile touching her mouth every so often. For the first time since they'd taken her, she didn't feel quite so helpless. They weren't as in control of her as they thought, and that gave her enormous satisfaction.

Five days later Alessandro Forli stood looking down at all of the photographs that had been taken of Cassie by her captors. In all of them she held a current newspaper.

Franco had studied the pictures until his eyes burned. And then it hit him. "Where's the first picture?" he asked Alessandro Forli, who was also staring at them.

Her grandfather pushed it across the desk. "What's the matter? What do you see?"

"Look at her hands in this one."

Her grandfather did, then shook his head. "I don't understand. She's simply holding up a newspaper."

"That's exactly right. And she's doing it the way anyone might. Now look at the second picture."

He lifted his shoulders. "So?"

"Look at her eyes. She's looking at her right hand, not at the camera. And look at her fingers. The hand she's looking at shows four fingers, the other one two. She's giving us numbers. Four and two. Four first because that's the one she's looking at."

Alessandro Forli narrowed his eyes on the picture. "How do you know she isn't signaling a six?

Franco pulled out another picture. "Look at this one. Instead of a hand on either side of the newspaper, she has both hands at the top showing four fingers on either hand, pushed together for the number eight." He was smiling for the first time in days. "She's doing it, Alessandro. She's telling us how to find her right under their noses." He lined up the pictures in their proper order and wrote down the results, then stared at them.

"What do you think they mean?" Cassie's grandfather asked.

Franco shook his head. "I don't know. It could be an address. A phone number."

Taddeo, who had been listening from across the room, walked over to the desk and looked down at the paper with the numbers on it. "Or a license-plate number," he suggested.

"That, too." Franco picked up the telephone and called the policeman in charge of the investigation and gave him the numbers. When he hung up he sat down in a chair across from Alessandro Forli. "He'll run it through their computer and get back to us."

"While we do the hard part." Her grandfather sighed.

"Yes, waiting."

The phone rang an hour later. Franco looked at Alessandro and took a deep breath before answering. When he hung up a smile lit his eyes. "It's a license-plate number. She did it."

"You don't have her back yet."

"I know that, but this is more than we've had before."

"The car could be stolen."

"If it was, the owners never reported it." He studied the older man for a long moment. "The police are going to the owner's address. I'm going with them. If you'd like to come, I'll drive you."

"That's generous of you, but I think not. I'd rather no one knew of my involvement, particularly the police. I'll wait to hear from you."

"All right. I'll call you either way." And then Franco left. When he got to the house, the police were already there in unmarked cars. A van parked in front bore a license plate with the number Cassie had given them.

Everyone sat and waited. Less than an hour later three people left the house and got into the van. Two police cars and Franco followed at a safe distance. They drove for about twenty minutes on a main highway, but then turned onto a dirt road that cut through the middle of a vineyard. The police didn't attempt to follow the car for fear of giving their presence away, and Franco stopped behind them.

Then the van reappeared. One of the police cars fell in behind it, but the other turned into the vineyard. Franco followed that one. The road led to a small utility building, with bars on its windows. There were no other cars around. They stopped some distance away from the building and then carefully sneaked up to it. Franco looked in one of the windows and saw nothing.

His heart sank. He'd been so sure that Cassie was there. Then he looked in the other window and saw her sitting on a cot, staring at a newspaper. She was safe. She was alive. He didn't notice the tears that coursed down his cheeks.

When he signaled to the police, they got an ax from the trunk of their car and began battering the door.

Cassie's heart stopped at the noise. Those people had just been there. Why had they come back? And why were they breaking down the door?

It flew open a moment later and two policemen entered. But the only person she saw was the man standing slightly behind them. Her eyes filled with tears, and then her whole face lit up as she threw herself into his arms. "I knew you'd figure it out!"

Chapter Ten

Franco held her to him as tightly as he could, reveling in having found her safe. He didn't want to let her go ever again. "Oh, Cassie," he breathed. "Are you all right?"

She pulled slightly away from him and nodded.

"Did they hurt you in any way?"

"They never touched me—or even spoke to me."

He cupped her face in his hands and gazed tenderly down at her. Then he wordlessly pulled her back into his arms. Cassie let herself lean on him, still not believing that it was all over.

"I'm taking you home," he said finally.

"But the police..."

"Can talk to you tomorrow. Right now you're mine and I'm not sharing you with anyone else for any reason." He spoke to the police in Italian, which Cassie didn't have the presence of mind to follow, then took her to his car. Cassie leaned back against the seat with a sigh she'd been saving up since her kidnapping, then turned to stare at Franco's profile as he drove. He looked over at her again and again, and finally he shook his head. "I don't know how I'm going to get us home. I'm afraid to take my eyes off you."

Cassie smiled. "Does Sam know what happened?"

"No. I left him at the school and the teachers kept him away from the television."

"Good. He's too young to have to deal with this." Cassie rubbed her temples. She had the beginnings of a very bad headache. "Did anything interesting happen while I was away? I feel as though I've been isolated on an island somewhere."

"Only one thing that you need to concern yourself with. Your custody of Sam came through. He's now legally yours."

Her eyes filled with quick tears that she blinked away almost as fast they came. "Thank you," she said softly. "We owe you more than we can ever possibly repay."

Franco pulled the car to a stop in front of the villa and turned to his wife. "Cassie, don't you know by now that I don't want repayment. I just want you. I want us to be a family."

Cassie warmed to his words. It was what she wanted, too. But how could it ever happen? For the first time since he'd found her, Cassie remembered what she had found out before her kidnapping. Alessandro Forli was her grandfather. A shadow crossed her face.

Franco reached out and tenderly cupped her cheek in his hand. "What is it? What's wrong?"

She put her hand over his and held it there for a moment, then turned her head slightly and rested her lips against his palm. "Nothing," she said finally. "Nothing that can't wait."

The front door of the villa opened and Maria and Taddeo came racing out to hug her as she stepped from the car.

But Franco stayed in the car watching the scene through the windshield, his eyes narrowed.

Cassie suddenly turned her head and met his gaze. Her mouth parted softly as though there were something she wanted to say to him, but she closed it again and turned away.

His eyes followed her into the villa. How was it possible to love a woman as much as he loved Cassie? For the first time, he understood the reason his father had committed suicide after his mother's murder. Franco had hated his father for so long for what he had perceived as his weakness. But if his father had felt for his mother even half what Franco felt for Cassie, the pain he had suffered when she died must have been unbearable. The solution his father had chosen wasn't one that he himself would choose, but when he thought about a life without Cassie, that life spread out before him in all its emptiness.

He rubbed his forehead and sat for a moment longer before taking the keys out of the ignition and walking across the drive and into the villa.

When she was finally alone in her room Cassie ran a hot bubble bath and sank into it up to her chin. She didn't want to think, but her mind wouldn't let her just lie there. She had some problems, and they needed to be faced. How was she going to tell Franco she was leaving? Because that was what she had to do. How was she going to look the man she loved in the eye and tell him good-bye? He could read her like an open book, and if he pressed her for her reasons for wanting to leave, she wasn't sure she could lie to him. The last thing she wanted was for him to realize that she knew who her grandfather was; he would immediately know that that was why she wanted the annulment. She couldn't stand by and watch his career be ruined.

Cassie soaked a while longer, her mind in a whirl. Then she got out of the bathtub and stood under the shower to wash her hair. When she finished, she toweled herself off and used a blow dryer on her hair until it fell silkily past her shoulders. It was wonderful to be clean again. Then she wrapped her long, white terry-cloth robe around herself and went into her room. She'd been in the bath longer than she'd realized. The sun had set and her bedroom was shrouded in darkness. Cassie turned on a table lamp next to her bed. A noise in Franco's room caught her ear. Now would be as good a time to talk to him as any. She started for the door, but stopped halfway there and stood staring at it. She couldn't.

But she had to. She forced herself toward it once more and opened it without knocking. Franco stood in front of his window staring outside, his hands in the pockets of his trousers. A dim light shone in a corner of the room. "Franco?"

He turned to look at her, then wordlessly crossed the room and pulled her into his arms. Cassie melted against him, then stiffened almost immediately. "We need to talk."

She felt him move his cheek against her hair. "No," he said softly. "No talking. We just need to be together." He held her even closer, and Cassie was lost. Then he moved her slightly away from himself and tilted her face toward his with a finger under her chin. His eyes lingered over every feature and finally came to rest on her mouth. He lowered his head to hers and captured her lips with devastating gentleness. Cassie moaned at the contact as a wave of passion shot through her, helpless to stop what was happening. How could she when she wanted him every bit as much as he wanted her? She wrapped her arms around his neck and pulled him closer as his tongue thrust deeply and suggestively into her mouth. His hands slid down her back to her hips and pulled her tightly against him. She felt his need and it aroused her even more. The belt of her robe fell to the floor and the robe itself followed shortly thereafter. Franco picked her up in his arms and carried her to the bed, then straightened and looked down at her. "Do you have any idea how beautiful you are to me?"

Cassie's breasts rose and lowered with her rapid breathing as she watched Franco take off his clothes. It seemed like an eternity before he was next to her, holding her body against his warm flesh, stroking her into a passion she hadn't realized she was capable of. He made her his again and again, and each time the release was as sweet as the first.

At last they lay facing each other, their bodies covered with a fine film of perspiration. Franco pushed Cassie's damp hair away from her cheek and gazed into her eyes. He didn't need to say anything. All the love he felt shone from his eyes. Cassie's heart ached with the knowledge that she had let things get out of hand, but she couldn't help it. She couldn't help loving him the way she did. She couldn't help wanting him the way she did. And those things would never change.

A tear slipped from the corner of her eye and Franco brushed it away with a gentle finger. "What's this?"

She shook her head and moved closer to him. "Not now."

A feeling of foreboding washed over him as he held Cassie in his arms. He didn't press her; he knew in his heart he wasn't going to like hearing what she had to say. He pulled the sheet up over both of them and they lay in absolute stillness for a long time. After a while Cassie's even breathing told him she was asleep. She must have been exhausted after all that had happened to her. He kissed the top of her head and pulled her a little closer to his heart.

Cassie spent the next two days talking to the police. The people who had taken her had been caught and jailed, so she didn't have to worry about them anymore. When all of the things relating to the kidnapping had been taken care of, Cassie finally went to see Alessandro Forli.

She stood looking through his office window, then turned when she heard him open the door.

"Hello, Cassie," he said quietly. "I'm glad you're safe."

"Thank you." Her eyes searched his face across the room. "And thank you for all your help in finding me—Grandfather."

His shoulders straightened. "You know?"

"The morning I came to see you and you weren't here, I went into your library."

He understood immediately. "The portrait."

"It's a perfect likeness of my mother." She moved across the room to stand in front of him. "Why didn't you tell me? You've obviously known since you saw me at the Pantheon."

"I didn't think it was something you needed to know."

That made her angry. "*You* didn't think it was something I needed to know? Something that concerned my life as closely as this and you decided that I didn't need to know about it?"

"I'm sorry, Cassie. The decision I made was obviously a bad one. But I was doing what I thought best by keeping our relationship from you. You already knew what I was. When your mother found out, she couldn't deal with it. She ran away when she was only seventeen and I never saw her again. I didn't want you to run away. In you I had a second chance. We were becoming friends." A silence fell between them. "You were beginning to like me, despite what you knew about me."

She couldn't argue with that.

He walked to his desk and took out a thin cigar from a drawer. "So," he said, looking back at her, "what are you going to do now?"

Cassie pushed her hair away from her face. "Sam and I are going back to Illinois tomorrow."

"Franco told me he was sending you there until this business with Genco ends."

"We're going to be staying there."

Her grandfather's eyes narrowed. "What about your husband?"

"I haven't talked to him about this yet, but I'm going to ask him to have the marriage annulled. Under the circumstances, and despite what's happened between us, I don't think there will be a problem with that."

"But why? The man is obviously in love with you, child."

"I'm not the right wife for him."

"Because of me—is that what you're saying?"

Cassie walked back to the window and leaned her shoulder against the frame as she looked out. "He can't very well be a special prosecutor if his wife is the granddaughter of the head of one of the largest crime families in Italy, can he?"

"But no one need ever know."

She shook her head. "It'll come out eventually. Things like this always do."

"He'll go back into private practice."

"That's what he said, but it isn't what he wants. It isn't where his heart is." She turned back to her grandfather. "He doesn't know that I've found out about you. I'd appreciate it if you didn't enlighten him. I want him to think I'm leaving for other reasons."

The old man didn't understand her request, but he agreed to it anyway. He lit his cigar and stared at her for a long, silent moment. "Are you going to cut me out of your life the way Elena did?"

Cassie still stood staring out the window. "No. You're my grandfather. You're Sam's grandfather. And, except for Aunt Emily, you're the only family we have left. I'd like Sam to have a chance to know you. You'll be welcome in our home in Illinois any time you care to visit, but I won't allow Sam to come here. I don't want him exposed to your...business."

"If those are your terms, I accept them."

She turned to him again and took a deep breath. "Thank you. Good-bye, Grandfather."

He didn't try to hug her, though his arms ached to. She wasn't ready for that yet. "Good-bye."

When she got home, Franco was waiting for her. She had managed to avoid him for two days, and he wasn't having another minute of it. He took her none too gently by the arm and pulled her into the library. "Where have you been?"

"Out."

He closed the door behind them and then turned to look at her. "You had something to tell me the other night and I didn't want to hear it. Well, I still don't want to hear it, but I guess it's time I did."

Cassie had to steel herself against the longing to be in his arms. "I guess it is at that." She looked directly into his eyes. "I'd like to go ahead with the annulment."

He stared at her. "What?"

Cassie swallowed. Hard. "I want an annulment."

He really didn't understand. But then, how could he? "Why, Cassie?"

She forced her eyes to remain locked with his. "I should think that would be obvious. I don't want to be married to you."

"And when did you decide that?"

"Sometime during the seven days I was being held in a utility shed."

Franco's jaw grew taut with the pain her words inflicted, and Cassie almost hated herself for what she was doing, but she couldn't let him give up everything for which he had worked so hard because of her.

Franco moved to stand in front of her and put his hands on her shoulders. "You love me, Cassie," he said softly.

For the first time, she dropped her gaze. "What I feel for you has nothing to do with this. And I really can't talk about it anymore. I'm sure you understand my reasons." She cleared her throat and looked at him again. "I want to thank you for all you've done for Sam and me. And good luck tomorrow. Taddeo tells me the Genco trial starts then."

He said nothing, and Cassie allowed herself the luxury of gazing at him. "Good-bye," she said softly, and barely made it out of the room before her tears fell.

Franco stared after her retreating back with a thoughtful frown. He didn't believe her for a moment. There was a lot more going on here than she was willing to tell him. He knew his Cassie well, and he would have bet everything he had that the kidnapping hadn't frightened her into wanting to leave him. With the Cassie he knew, it would only have served to make her more determined to stay.

But for now he let her go. It was for the best, at least until the Genco trial was over. But she hadn't seen the last of him. And if she thought for one moment that he was going to start annulment proceedings, she was dead wrong. Cassie was his and she was going to stay that way.

Four months later Cassie waved to Sam as he drove off with his friend Jason and Jason's father. This time they were going to a football game. She rubbed her arms against the cold winter air and looked out over the snow-covered pastures—Franco's snow-covered pastures. She had left the deed to the Illinois property with him in Rome and had been sending him monthly rental checks.

Four months. She went back inside and sat on the floor in the living room, poking at the fire. Four lonely, interminable months. If it hadn't been for Sam and the need to keep up a happy front when he was around, she didn't know what she would have done. She had thought that not being with Franco would get easier as time passed, but it wasn't working out that way. She lay awake for hours at night, praying for sleep so that, for a little while at least, she wouldn't be thinking about him, wouldn't be aching to be back in his arms.

She hadn't heard from him once since they'd returned to Illinois. She hadn't really expected to. Taddeo called her every so often and had even come for a short visit. From him she knew that the Genco trial had ended a week before and that he had been convicted.

There was a knock at the door. Cassie walked back into the foyer and opened it, and her eyes grew wide even as her heart leaped at the sight of the man standing before her. "Franco!"

"Hello, Cassie," he said without smiling.

She moved aside to let him in, then closed the door after him. "What are you doing here?"

"Completing some unfinished business between us."

"The annulment?"

His eyes were on her lovely face. "The marriage." His mouth came down on hers and Cassie was taken completely by surprise. Her lips parted softly beneath his as she melted against him. But as soon as she realized what was happening, she tried to push herself away from him. Franco looked unsmilingly into her eyes as his arms held her close. "No, Cassie. No more."

This time when his mouth came down on hers she moaned softly and wrapped her arms around his neck. She was completely lost in him; there was no denying the passion he could arouse in her.

This time it was he who pulled away to gaze tenderly down at her. "You shouldn't be so surprised. Did you really think I'd let you leave me for good?"

"It's been four months."

"That's how long the trial took." He removed his coat and threw it over a chair in the foyer. "I spoke to Alessandro Forli last week. He had an interesting story to tell me."

Cassie lowered her eyes. "He wasn't supposed to say anything."

"Even though he knew what you were doing couldn't have been more wrong? What kind of grandfather would that make him?"

"One of his word."

Franco shook his head. "He did the right thing, Cassie. And the moment he told me, everything fell into place. You didn't leave me because you were frightened that something else might happen to you. You left me because you loved me. And I love you. The two of us belong together. Do you honestly think I care more about my damn career than I care about you?"

"No." Her eyes pleaded with his for understanding. "But I didn't think you could ever be completely happy without doing the work you love, either, and I didn't want to be responsible for that."

"Oh, Cassie," he said softly, shaking his head. "Don't you know that the only thing that gives my life meaning is you? Without you there's nothing."

A tear ran down Cassie's cheek. "I love you, too."

He kissed the tear away and looked deeply into her eyes. "We've got some problems, and I'm not trying to gloss them over. They're important ones, but they're not insurmountable. As of last week I'm back in private practice. If something I can't resist comes up and a special prosecutor is needed, I'll take it, but it won't be my life anymore. I don't want it to be my life anymore."

Franco pulled her into his arms. "You and I belong together. We always have and we always will. And if that means that we live part of the year in Italy and part of the year in Illinois, then that's what we'll do."

Cassie closed her eyes and surrendered herself completely. How could she ever have thought that she could live without him? She ached to be near him, to touch him, to love him. He was the only man she could ever love.

And she knew why. He was no ordinary man, and he was hers and hers alone.

The Silhouette
Cameo Tote Bag
Now available
for just $6.99

Handsomely designed in blue and bright pink, its stylish good looks make the Cameo Tote Bag an attractive acces-
sory. The Cameo Tote Bag is big and roomy (13″ square), with reinforced handles and a snap-shut top. You can buy the Cameo Tote Bag for $6.99, plus $1.50 for post-age and handling.

Send your name and address with check or money order for $6.99 (plus $1.50 postage and handling), a total of $8.49 to:

> **Silhouette Books**
> **120 Brighton Road**
> **P.O. Box 5084**
> **Clifton, NJ 07015-5084**
> **ATTN: Tote Bag**

SIL—T—1

The Silhouette Cameo Tote Bag can be pur-chased pre-paid only. No charges will be accep-ted. Please allow 4 to 6 weeks for delivery.

Arizona and N.Y. State Residents Please Add Sales Tax

Offer not available in Canada.

Take 4 Silhouette Special Edition novels
FREE

and preview future books in your home for 15 days!

When you take advantage of this offer, you get 4 Silhouette Special Edition® novels FREE and without obligation. Then you'll also have the opportunity to preview 6 brand-new books —delivered right to your door for a FREE 15-day examination period—as soon as they are published.

When you decide to keep them, you pay just $1.95 each ($2.50 each in Canada) *with no shipping, handling, or other charges of any kind!*

Romance *is* alive, well and flourishing in the moving love stories of Silhouette Special Edition novels. They'll awaken your desires, enliven your senses, and leave you tingling all over with excitement...and the first 4 novels are yours to keep. You can cancel at any time.

As an added bonus, you'll also receive a FREE subscription to the Silhouette Books Newsletter as long as you remain a member. Each issue is filled with news on upcoming books, interviews with your favorite authors, even their favorite recipes.

To get your 4 FREE books, fill out and mail the coupon today!

Silhouette Special Edition®

Silhouette Books, 120 Brighton Rd., P.O. Box 5084, Clifton, NJ 07015-5084

Clip and mail to: Silhouette Books,
120 Brighton Road, P.O. Box 5084, Clifton, NJ 07015-5084 *

YES. Please send me 4 FREE Silhouette Special Edition novels. Unless you hear from me after I receive them, send me 6 new Silhouette Special Edition novels to preview each month. I understand you will bill me just $1.95 each, a total of $11.70 (in Canada, $2.50 each, a total of $15.00), with no shipping, handling, or other charges of any kind. There is no minimum number of books that I must buy, and I can cancel at any time. The first 4 books are mine to keep.

BS18R6

Name	(please print)

Address		Apt. #

City	State/Prov.	Zip/Postal Code

* In Canada, mail to: Silhouette Canadian Book Club, 320 Steelcase Rd., E., Markham, Ontario, L3R 2M1, Canada
Terms and prices subject to change.
SILHOUETTE SPECIAL EDITION is a service mark and registered trademark.   SE-SUB-1

COMING NEXT MONTH

PLEASE STAND BY—Marie Nicole
Cartoonist Dirk Kilpatrick had created "Abby," the perfect woman.
No one could compete with her...until he met Vinnie. She had all
Abby's charms, with one advantage...she was real.

FORGOTTEN LOVE—Phyllis Halldorson
Could love conquer all? Mercy's husband, Morgan, had lost his
memory, and she was a stranger to him. Perhaps wrapped in her
arms he would remember the love they'd shared.

THE MATTHEWS AFFAIR—Victoria Glenn
Denise's past had left her as skittish as a colt when it came to love,
but Logan wouldn't give up. Slowly he aimed to win her heart.

WITH MARRIAGE IN MIND—Dorothy Cork
Noeline Hastings had resigned herself to marrying her reliable but
boring boyfriend, Andrew. Then she met Justin Fitzroy and realized
that she could never settle for another man.

THE SEA AT DAWN—Laurie Paige
Roth wasn't the kind of man to fall for a woman like Melba. He
was rich and powerful. He wouldn't be attracted to a sensible,
down-to-earth girl...or would he?

CAMERA SHY—Lynnette Morland
Calm, cool and unerringly professional, Carla Copeland had met
her match. Fletcher Arendt sensed the passion lurking beneath her
facade, and he planned to find a way to unleash it.

AVAILABLE NOW:

NO ORDINARY MAN
Brittany Young

A TASTE OF ROMANCE
Glenda Sands

VIRTUE AND VICE
Lucy Gordon

A WOMAN'S WILES
Nora Powers

A FRIEND OR TWO
Debbie Macomber

SWEET GEORGIA GAL
Emilie Richards